A CASE OF PERPLEXITY IN PICCADILLY

A Freddy Pilkington-Soames Adventure 7

CLARA BENSON

MOUNT
STREET
PRESS

A Case of Perplexity in Piccadilly

West End theatre impresario Septimus Gooch is a man with many enemies, but when he's found dead in his leading lady's dressing-room the police put it down to an accident.

The cast of Septimus's latest musical production at the Jollity Theatre are having none of it, however—this is the second mysterious death in two months, and they're convinced Septimus died after being frightened out of his wits by the ghost that's haunted the theatre ever since it burned to the ground many years ago. A malevolent spirit is on the loose, striking them down one by one. Which of them will be next?

Press-man Freddy Pilkington-Soames was backstage at the Jollity on the night Septimus died. He doesn't believe in ghosts, but he knows a suspicious death when he sees one— and when a third person dies there's no doubt this time that a human hand was behind it.

Freddy's fending off the attentions of several chorus-girls at once, so has his own distractions to contend with. But murder's no joke, and he'll do anything he can to catch the killer before the whole production falls apart.

After all, the show must go on.

———

Sign up to my mailing list at clarabenson.com/newsletter.

Dramatis Personae

THEATRE PEOPLE

Septimus Gooch: Theatrical producer and owner of the Jollity Theatre

Jenny Minter: His estranged wife, a respected actress and singer

Max D'Auberville: Writer and producer of intellectual plays

Loveday Curtis: Ambitious female lead of *Have At It!*

Rupert St. Clair: Handsome tenor and male lead of *Have At It!*

Trenton Bagshawe: A young man of theatrical bent

Desirée Oliver: Ingenue

Morry Jinks: A comedian

Bert Spooner: A comedian

Peggy Lupton: Member of the chorus

Minnie Monteith: Member of the chorus

Maudie Monteith: Member of the chorus

Dinah Belmonte: Member of the chorus

Joyce: Member of the chorus

Artie Jennings: Stage-manager at the Jollity

Alf: Stage door-keeper at the Jollity

Alice: A dresser

Cyril Payne: Carpenter and man-of-all-work

OTHER CHARACTERS

Freddy Pilkington-Soames: Our hero

Lady Gertrude 'Gertie' McAloon: Bright young thing

Biffy Burfoot: A well-connected young man

Lord Oakford: A concerned father

Mr. Bickerstaffe: Editor of the *Clarion*

Sir Aldridge Featherstone: Owner of the *Clarion*

Lady Featherstone: His wife

Mrs. Marjorie Belcher: His sister

Jolliffe: A well-behaved reporter

Detective Inspector Entwistle of Scotland Yard

Detective Sergeant Bird of Scotland Yard

Prologue

FROM THE *CLARION* OF TUESDAY, 9th September, 1930:

SUDDEN DEATH OF CHORUS-DANCER

Theatre thought to be haunted

An inquest into the death of Miss Una Joan Bryant, 18, who was found dead in her dressing-room at the Jollity Theatre, was opened yesterday at Westminster Coroner's Court.

She had been expected on stage for the second act of the evening performance of *Have At It!* starring Loveday Curtis and Rupert St. Clair, but failed to appear on cue, and the show went on without her. After the performance ended she was found lying lifeless on the floor of the dressing-room shared by the members of the chorus. A doctor was summoned, but was unable to revive her, and the girl was pronounced dead. There was no indication that she had met with an accident of any kind.

The mother of the deceased, Mrs. Mary Bryant, of

Grove Street, Birmingham, said her daughter had been sickly as a child, and the doctor had advised that she be sent to dancing classes to strengthen her constitution. The prescription had worked, and her daughter had improved so far in health over the years as to be able to embark upon a career as a professional dancer. Mrs. Bryant stated that her daughter wrote every week, and would certainly have mentioned it had she been feeling unwell or uneasy about her health in any way.

Mr. Arthur Jennings, the stage-manager at the Jollity Theatre, said there had been some agitation among certain members of the cast of *Have At It!* as a rumour was going around that the theatre was haunted. There was a tendency to superstition among members of the theatrical profession, and despite his efforts to discourage all such speculation, he had not been able to prevent the view from taking hold that Miss Bryant had been frightened to death by an apparition.

Miss Loveday Curtis was then called. She disagreed with Mr. Jennings' assertion that talk of a ghost was mere superstition. The Jollity Theatre had burned down many years ago, and it was common knowledge that the theatre was haunted by the ghost of an actor who had died in the fire. She herself had heard ghostly voices on several occasions in her dressing-room, and despite what Mr. Jennings said, she was sure that a spectral presence had appeared before Miss Bryant and caused her to die of terror.

Miss Peggy Lupton, a member of the chorus who was first to find the body, said that Miss Bryant had seemed well on the evening of the incident, and had not confided any worries to her. She had no idea what could have caused the girl's death. She had heard the rumours of a ghost, but did not believe in such things herself. She had never heard any voices or seen an apparition of any kind.

Dr. H. B. Hales, who made the post-mortem examination of the body of Miss Bryant, said he had observed some signs of a heart defect, in that the heart was slightly enlarged, but there was nothing otherwise to show how the girl had died.

Coroner—Might she have been frightened to death, as Miss Curtis suggested?

Doctor—Certainly not by anything in the corporeal world. However, since my sphere of expertise is the purely physiological and I am not qualified to comment on matters pertaining to the after-life, if this hearing intends to descend into the realm of the supernatural then perhaps a clergyman might be more fit to answer that question. (Laughter.)

An open verdict was returned.

A small crowd was gathered outside the coroner's court to wait for Miss Curtis, who signed autographs as she came out.

Chapter One

AT THREE O'CLOCK on Monday Rupert St. Clair, smooth-skinned tenor over whom many a breathless female theatre-goer had palpitated for more years than the world cared to remember, visited Septimus Gooch at his London flat to talk about the tour of the provinces which was planned for Septimus's latest musical production *Have At It!* once its London run had finished. A manservant admitted Rupert and ushered him silently into the study, where Septimus was sitting at a large desk, writing. He did not look up when the visitor came in, but went on writing.

'Have you seen the piece about me in the *Herald*?' said Rupert. 'Rather flattering, don't you think?'

Septimus grunted but made no reply.

'It's all going marvellously well, and ought to go across splendidly outside London. As a matter of fact, that's why I'm here. I was talking to Loveday yesterday, and she says she's already received her contract. When am I to get mine?'

Septimus signed his name with a flourish and put down his pen.

'I'm not renewing your contract,' he said.

'What do you mean?'

'Just what I say. I've my eye on someone else for your part.'

Rupert went pale.

'But—but why?'

'You're not the young man you were. It's time you stepped aside and let someone else take the rôle—someone nearer the age of the character.'

'Thirty-five isn't old!' exclaimed Rupert, who in fact was nearer forty-five.

'You've fluffed that high D sharp three times out of four lately, Jennings tells me.'

'I had a cold all last week,' said Rupert. 'It's much better now.'

'I've heard you myself—you can't hit the notes any more. It happens to the best of us. Your contract goes to the end of the London run but after that I suggest you start making other arrangements. I have a couple of character parts coming up if you'd like to try for them.'

Rupert St. Clair had certain financial commitments and an expensive lifestyle, and had been doing his best to avoid looking reality in the face for some time. Now it slapped him across both cheeks in quick succession. He was horrified.

'You can't do this! I'll—'

'You'll what? Go somewhere else, is that it? Who'll take you on with your habits? I hired you out of the goodness of my heart, but business is business, and if you can't stand the pace then it's time you stepped aside and let someone else have a turn.'

Rupert had turned from white to red during this speech. He swallowed and clenched his fists, then opened his mouth to speak, but before he could say a word Septimus rang a bell and the manservant appeared silently.

'Show Mr. St. Clair out,' said Septimus.

———

A Case of Perplexity in Piccadilly

ON TUESDAY AT ELEVEN O'CLOCK, Miss Desirée Oliver stood on the deserted stage of the Jollity Theatre, marking out in her head the movements of a particularly complicated number which closed the first act of *Have At It!* Desirée was a recent and very keen addition to the performing world, who had yet to make a name for herself and was determined that if hard work could do it, then she should not be found wanting. At present she was occupying the supporting rôle of Loveday Curtis's sister—a part which she had won on the strength of her extraordinarily sweet singing voice—and had recently been appointed as understudy to Miss Curtis herself.

She finished marking out the movements on stage, then since she was there she decided she might as well warm up her voice and rehearse her little solo number for which she had received praise in several of the London papers. She ran through the first verse once, then hummed the chorus as she practised a change to the dance they had agreed earlier that week, and finally ran through the whole song, unaccompanied and without a mistake. She was just about to try it again when she heard someone clapping from the wings, and she whirled around to see Septimus Gooch walking onto the stage towards her. Desirée regarded him with some trepidation.

'That wasn't bad at all,' said Septimus. 'But don't forget in the second chorus you need to be standing here next to the mast so that Bagshawe can reach to hand you the dagger from his position in the rigging. Otherwise, he's just hanging there waiting like a fool.'

'Oh, yes, I'm sorry, I forgot. Like this.' Desirée did as he said.

'That's it. Take the dagger. Now pretend I'm St. Clair. Twirl around and hand it to me.'

Desirée twirled obediently, stumbled a little and somehow found herself being clasped in Septimus Gooch's arms. She went bright pink, gave a squeak, and tried to extricate herself. He kept tight hold of her.

'Remember what I told you,' he said. 'You can do better than this. You want to be famous, don't you?'

She nodded, despite herself.

'Well, then, there's a short-cut if you choose to take it.'

She went even pinker and wrenched herself free, straightening her frock as she stared at him, rather as a lamb might gaze helplessly at a ravenous wolf.

'But I'm not—' she began.

'Don't tell me you're not that kind of girl. I've been in this business thirty years or more, and let me tell you, when it comes to getting parts they're all that kind of girl. You might as well play the game, you know, since everyone thinks you're doing it anyway.'

'They don't!' Desirée exclaimed, aghast.

'Besides, I know all about you,' he went on. 'You've been keeping a little secret from us all, haven't you?'

'What?'

Septimus put his hand into his inside pocket and brought out a scrap of paper, which he held up.

'Who'd have thought it, eh?' he said.

Desirée's face went from pink to white in a moment and she drew in her breath.

'Where did you get that?'

'A friend of mine in the North who came to see the show a couple of weeks ago sent it to me. He thought I'd be interested to see it. I certainly was.'

She attempted defiance.

'Well, what of it?'

'What of it? I don't know what you're playing at, but I guess the stage is a dream of yours. I could speak up any time I liked and all this would be over for you.'

'You wouldn't, would you? Please don't!'

'Not so precious now, are you, Miss Hoity-Toity?'

Septimus's small black eyes glittered and his voice held a note of menace. There came the sound of voices offstage. The stage-manager and some of the stage-hands had arrived. Desirée backed away then turned to leave. Septimus Gooch raised his voice and called after her as she almost ran into the wings.

'Just you think about what I said. Remember—a word from me and you'll never set foot on a stage again!'

————

ON WEDNESDAY LUNCH-TIME MORRY JINKS, the shorter, wider half of that well-known comedic duo Jinks and Spooner (catch-phrase: 'You'll Kackle at their Krazy Kapers!'), ran Septimus Gooch to earth at his regular eating-place in Soho. He sat down at Septimus's table without being invited and set his jaw in the manner of one who is determined not to be put off.

'Have you had time to think about what I said yet?' he asked abruptly.

Septimus unhurriedly finished chewing his food, took a gulp of wine and patted his mouth with his napkin.

'I have,' he replied.

'Well?'

Septimus took another mouthful of wine and eyed two smart young women who had just entered the establishment. He watched as the waiter sat them at a table by the window, then at last turned to Jinks.

'There's nothing doing.'

The colour rose in Jinks's cheeks. It was not in his nature to be conciliatory, but he knew the importance of treading carefully in this instance, so he bit back the epithet that had sprung to his lips and forced himself to remain calm.

'Look, I know Bert was a bit rude to you—'

'He was downright insubordinate. To my face and behind my back. Don't think I don't know what goes on when I'm not there.'

'Well, that's as may be,' said Jinks. 'But then why insist on keeping me on after he's gone? The show isn't the same with just the one of us. You know it and the audience knows it. I don't get half the laughs alone as we would together. We're a double act. The famous Jinks and Spooner.'

'Not so famous lately. You're a bit past it these days. There are newer acts coming up now that are getting more attention.'

Jinks gritted his teeth.

'Well then, take one of them on. The show will be better for it, and me and Bert'll be better for it. Look, I'll be straight with you, Mr. Gooch: we've had an offer to go to New York with the Joe Barber Troupe. There's a contract at the Hippodrome—twelve shows a week for six months and more if it goes down well. It could be huge. We've been trying to get to America for a long time, only they sail in a few weeks so we have to give an answer quick. I'd never have signed that contract if I'd realized it meant you could tie me into a job separate from Bert. It was an honest mistake. Won't you let me out early? It's only a couple of months, and you could fill the part easy as winking.'

Septimus was absorbed in lighting a cigar, and Jinks had to repeat the question. He waited in an agony of suspense as Septimus eyed him and seemed to consider the matter.

'You need to know that you can't just do anything you like,' he said at last. 'I won't be crossed. You need to learn some respect. You'll do the run and like it.'

'But—'

'The answer's no.'

'You'll regret this,' said Jinks in a fury.

'I doubt it,' replied Septimus dismissively, and gestured to the waiter for the bill.

ON THURSDAY AT TEN, Max D'Auberville, known to the theatre world as the writer and producer of the wildly successful play *Far Hope* (and a number of more recent efforts which had been rather less successful, but which he preferred not to mention) was on the stage of the Calliope Theatre with his stage-manager, running through some last-minute changes to his latest production, when he looked up to see Septimus Gooch standing in the front row of the auditorium, gazing about him with mild interest. D'Auberville hid his dismay and walked across to the front of the stage.

'Septimus, old boy!' he exclaimed, with every appearance of pleasure. 'I was just going to come and see you.'

'Were you, now? And here's me thinking you'd been avoiding me.'

'No, no, not at all!' said D'Auberville, with desperate joviality.

Septimus came up onto the stage and started picking up props and putting them down, tapping the scenery and examining it as though assessing the value of everything. The stage-manager glanced from Septimus to his employer, and if he noticed a slight tremble in D'Auberville's hands and a touch of perspiration at his brow which gave the lie to his confident manner, he was discreet enough not to stare.

'Going well, then, is it, this new thing of yours?' inquired Septimus.

'*Ravens?* Oh, it's going to do marvellously, you'll see!' replied D'Auberville. 'Why, I had Roper of the *Evening Chronicle* here for an early peek this week, and he was practically falling over himself to praise it. "Max," he said, "if you haven't a hit on your hands then I'm a Dutchman!"'

'When does it open? Saturday, isn't it?'

'That's right. We're already booked solid for four weeks.'

Septimus grunted.

'Could be worse, after the last two disasters. By the way, any news for me on that front?'

'Ah, yes—about that,' said D'Auberville easily. 'I was wondering whether you mightn't consider granting a short extension on the loan. You see, what with one thing and another, I'm a trifle behind-hand. A couple of months and I'm almost certain—I *am* certain—that I'll have the money for you, but cash is a little tight at the moment. You know how things are in the early days of a new play, and there were one or two hitches in rehearsals which took some money to put right, so if you could see your way clear…'

'A couple of months? But you're only booked for four weeks. What if the takings drop off?'

'Oh, they won't, you can be sure of that. I've never been more certain of anything.'

'That's what you said with *Dry Harvest*, and that other one with the French title, but they both folded after six weeks.'

'Well, I mean, yes, but—'

Septimus cut him short.

'I've been waiting long enough for that money. You'd better get it, and quickly. I've had enough of your excuses.'

Max stared at him. Septimus was standing under a large piece of heavy scenery which was swaying dangerously overhead. If it fell it would crush him to death. Perhaps aware of the danger, Septimus strolled out from under the scenery and came to stand close to Max, looking him straight in the eye. Both men were of tall and commanding presence, but there was no doubt which of them had the upper hand at this moment.

'I want that money, Max. You've got until the 27th.'

'But I can't get it by the 27th,' pleaded D'Auberville. 'It'll bankrupt me.'

'Then you're in trouble,' said Septimus simply.

―――――

FRIDAY EVENING FOUND Loveday Curtis sitting before the glass in her dressing-room at the Jollity Theatre, her make-up half done. Her hand, holding a sponge coated in a vivid cosmetic preparation, was arrested in mid-air, and she was regarding Septimus Gooch's reflection behind her, an expression of dismay on her face.

'What do you mean, you're not going to divorce Jenny?'

'There's no need,' said Septimus. 'Neither of us is interested in remarrying, so it would be a lot of trouble and scandal for nothing.'

'You're not interested in remarrying? But what about me?'

'What about you?'

'We're getting married, aren't we?'

'Who told you that?'

'You did,' said Loveday.

'No I didn't. I never said anything of the sort. I let you talk and didn't contradict you.'

'What? But why?'

'I knew nothing would dislodge the idea from that head of yours, and I'm not interested in rows.'

From the very earliest days of her life Loveday had been accustomed to getting her own way. She stared uncomprehendingly at Septimus.

'But we're supposed to be getting married,' she repeated. 'You don't want Jenny. Everyone knows you've been separated for years.'

'Only as man and wife. We get along all right, Jenny and I, and I want to leave her the business when I'm gone. She's a good head on her shoulders and will run it well. Besides, perhaps we'll make it up one day. She's still a good-looking woman—and she's not as expensive as you are.'

All at once Loveday saw the writing on the wall. She did not take his threats to resume married life with Jenny seriously, for what man would want a woman close on fifty when he could have one nearer twenty? But it could not be denied that he had become a little inattentive lately, and more than once she had seen him glancing at her understudy. She did not think Desirée was aware of it, but she knew Septimus well, and was certain it could be only a matter of time before he made his advances. Loveday had become accustomed to the finer things in life: the flowers, the little gifts of jewellery, the fashionable restaurants, and she had no wish to see them come to an end. It was necessary to act immediately.

She stood up and went to stand close to him. Even with only half her face made up she was obviously a very beautiful woman, and she took full advantage of the fact now. She gave him the tilted-head glance from under her lashes which had made her name and had regularly put her face in all the popular papers for the past year.

'You don't really mean it, do you?' she purred. 'Why, we're simply made for each other! You said so yourself just yesterday. Don't you remember?'

She made as if to put her arms around his neck, but he grimaced and pushed her away. The shove was unexpected and more violent than was necessary; Loveday staggered back with a little shriek, tripped over her make-up stool and almost fell over. It was undignified and almost comical—but there was nothing comical about the look on her face, which was pure poison.

'You've strung me along all this time,' she hissed. 'Well, I'm not going to let you get away with it. If you won't keep your promise then I'll—I'll—'

'Go on,' said Septimus, affecting an expression of mild interest.

Loveday was furious, but understood the wisdom of not burning her bridges. She had always been able to wind men around her finger, and she was sure Septimus was no exception. She recovered herself with an effort.

'You'll marry me or no-one,' she said.

Chapter Two

IT WAS a Saturday night in late October, and all of London
had taken advantage of a spell of unseasonably mild, dry
weather to throng in great numbers into the West End of the
city, its eating and drinking establishments and its palaces of
entertainment. Out in the streets people strolled to and fro,
groups of friends laughed together, taxis drew up outside
restaurants and disgorged cargoes of passengers attired in glit-
tering array, while strains of lively music emanated from the
open doors of brightly-lit locales, a siren call to lure in people
from the street and add to the general atmosphere of gaiety
and frivolity.

One who did not share the mood was Freddy Pilkington-
Soames, star reporter (as he liked to term himself) of the
Clarion, that beacon of decency and honesty which strove daily
to shine the light of revelation from the lofty heights of Fleet
Street into the murky depths of the metropolis. Having been
pushed into the job by his mother three years earlier, Freddy
had found himself unaccountably enjoying the life of a press-
man, for it had introduced him to many interesting people
and places and provided him with unusual experiences that
served to refresh his jaded palate, dispel the hopeless ennui

that would otherwise have been his fate in life, and give him a sense of purpose. The disadvantage of working for a living, however, was that it required him to engage his efforts at times when he would rather have been doing other things. This particular evening, for example, he had been called upon to write a review of a new play, *Consider the Ravens*, which was supposed to be very clever and allegorical but which promised dullness in equal measure to its fearsome erudition. To make matters worse, he had been instructed to act as escort to the wife and the sister of the *Clarion*'s owner, Sir Aldridge Feather- stone, who were very keen themselves to see the play. Sir Aldridge himself was unable to attend, and so the burden of responsibility had fallen upon Freddy, who was one of the few of Sir Aldridge's employees presentable enough to blend in smoothly with the *haut monde* of London.

Freddy had no objection to the theatre in itself, but his tastes ran to the lighter sort of spectacle, and the idea of sitting through three hours of earnest exposition without any jugglers or performing animals to liven things up did not fill him with enthusiasm. Moreover, he resented having to behave himself of a Saturday night—especially since Sir Aldridge's sister, Mrs. Marjorie Belcher, was an enthusiastic upholder of the Temperance cause, which meant that he could not even relieve the three hours of tedium and numb the stiffness that was only to be had from the seats of the Calliope Theatre with a drink or two in the interval. In addition, he had been forced to break off a previously arranged engagement with a young lady in whom he had a particular interest. He had invited Gertie to be one of the party, but she had snorted and informed him at length and in no uncertain terms that: 1) she would rather tear out her own eyes than sit for hours in front of that sort of bilge; 2) she was exceedingly miffed that he hadn't had the wit to think of a ready excuse to get out of it; and 3) he had jolly well better make it up to her later.

Here he was, then, with Lady Featherstone and Mrs.

Belcher, in among an earnest-looking crowd outside the Calliope Theatre, and with the prospect of a long evening ahead of him. Next door was the Jollity Theatre, currently showing *Have At It!*, a light musical entertainment which Freddy had seen and enjoyed a week or two earlier. There was already a crowd outside, and the atmosphere was one of great cheer, in stark contrast to the queue of serious theatre-goers outside the Calliope. Freddy regarded the lively scene enviously, but there was no escape from his duties, for the doors had opened and they were now being admitted. Freddy, on his best behaviour, took charge of the tickets, saw to the ladies' coats, and procured the programmes, then they all stood in conversation as Freddy did his best to entertain. Lady Featherstone pointed out a tall man of great presence standing nearby who she said was the producer of the play, Max D'Auberville, and they watched him with interest until it was time to go to their seats. The tickets had been bought at the last minute, and since it was a fashionable new production it had been impossible to get three places together. Lady Featherstone and Mrs. Belcher were therefore accommodated in two adjacent seats with a reasonable view, while Freddy was placed on the end of a row much further back, behind a woman wearing a large hat. This was an annoyance, but Freddy consoled himself for his poor view of the stage with the thought that since he was also well hidden from the sight of Lady Featherstone and Mrs. Belcher, at least he would not have to pretend to pay rapt attention for the whole play. Further considerations very quickly presented themselves, and he toyed with them idly in his head.

At seven o'clock prompt, the lights went down and there was a brief buzz of anticipation from the audience before the curtain ascended upon a bare stage and the play began. His half-formed idea having coalesced into specific intent, Freddy gave it a minute then rose silently from his seat, made his way out of the auditorium and emerged into the street. Five minutes later he was sitting in a comfortable front circle seat at the Jollity Theatre, and settling himself down to enjoy the evening performance of *Have At It!* He had taken care to inform himself of the approximate time of the interval at the Calliope, and was confident that provided he returned and showed his face at the expected moment, nobody would ever discover the deception.

At first, all went according to plan. The show was a good one, set alternately on a pirate ship and an island in the South Seas with a ruthless disregard for historical or geographical accuracy. It had witty dialogue, rousing and tuneful music played by a lively orchestra, hilarious routines from a well-known comedian, and several colourful and acrobatic dance numbers performed by a chorus of pretty girls dressed in impractical and abbreviated pirate costumes which would have caused them to catch their death of cold had they been so unwise as to wear them at sea. Freddy enjoyed it all immensely. Shortly before half past eight he left his seat, returned to the Calliope in time for the interval and played the part of a serious critic of high-brow drama. He listened carefully for cues from his companions, then set himself to talk at random but with apparent expertise about the use of metaphor and allegory in the first half of the play. The ladies frowned and nodded in agreement at his profound understanding of the Biblical allusions inherent in the deeper nature of one character in particular, and Lady Featherstone said the earlier scenes had reminded her somewhat of Book 5 of *Paradise Lost*, and Freddy said he was quite of her opinion, and had she caught the reference to Blake's *Job and His Daughters* in the tableau at the end of the first act? Then they all returned to the auditorium, and the lights went down for the second act, and Freddy once more rose from his seat and hurried back to the Jollity.

Here he found that the interval had just begun. He pondered the possibility of a drink, then was struck by another idea. Among the cast of *Have At It!* was Trenton Bagshawe, second son of the late Bishop of Tewkesbury and the brother of a friend of Freddy's. Trenton's foray onto the stage had not been especially well-received on the part of his family, who, despite all indications to the contrary, considered the whole business as an eccentric episode which he would soon grow out of. Trenton had invited Freddy, as a representative of the Press possibly worth cultivating, to come and see him back-stage whenever he liked. *Consider the Ravens* was not due to end until twenty past ten. Now seemed as good a moment as any to take advantage of the invitation. Freddy left the Jollity by the front entrance and turned down the little alley which separated it from the Calliope, heading for the stage door. He opened it and looked in.

'Hallo?' he called.

The stage door-keeper's box was empty. Freddy went in, and was preparing to pass through the entrance-lobby into the corridor beyond when the door-keeper himself turned up, a wiry man of sixty or so with a morose expression and a perpetual wheeze.

'Hallo, Alf,' said Freddy, who was not unknown at the stage doors of London. 'I'm here to see Trenton. He said I was to be admitted.'

'Did he, now?' said Alf. 'Well, he oughter known better, didn't he?'

Just then, a voice exclaimed, 'Freddy, old chap!' and Freddy looked up to see Trenton Bagshawe popping his head in, his face heavily made up. 'Let him in, Alf. I'll make it all right with Mr. Gooch.'

Ignoring Alf's protestations, he hustled Freddy down a narrow passage and into a dressing-room which proved to be little more than a cupboard strewn with clothes, shoes and other impedimenta. A half-smoked cigar rested in an ash-tray on a small table, next to a nearly empty bottle of whisky, two glasses, and a heap of old film magazines and copies of *The*

Stage. On a coat stand in the corner hung the usual array of outdoor clothes, as well as a brightly striped jester's costume, a pompadour wig and a fez. A large looking-glass covered one wall, with in front of it a dressing-table scattered about with bottles and boxes of grease-paints and powders.

'Won't be a mo,' said Trenton, and went out.

Freddy looked for somewhere to sit, but all the available chairs were occupied by piles of detritus. The wall was over-spread with photographs of actors who had played at the Jollity in the past, and he went across to examine them more closely. He read the names with interest—Lancelot Lovell, Adelaide Gilbert, The Great Alphonso—performers of a bygone era famous in their time, many of them no longer well-known to the public. Freddy was chuckling at the huge, old-fashioned moustache on an enormously fat man named Sylvester Ramsbottom, whose speciality appeared to be the unicycle, when his attention was caught by the sound of a man's raised voice proceeding along the corridor outside. It came closer, and Freddy heard the furious words 'You'll pay for this!' followed by the slamming of a door. He raised his eyebrows. A minute or two later Trenton came half into the room, still talking to someone out of sight. He made a gesture of acknowledgment to Freddy, and went on to his invisible companion:

'No, but look, my pal's here. Come in and meet him.'

He came into the room properly, followed by a pretty girl Freddy recognized as having played the sister of the leading lady.

'First-rate show, old thing,' Freddy said.

Trenton beamed.

'Do you like it? I hoped you would. Desirée, this is Freddy. He's at the *Clarion.*'

'Oh!' said Desirée, eyeing Freddy with interest.

'Desirée's going to be the next big sensation,' Trenton continued. Desirée blushed and disclaimed the compliment.

'I liked your song,' Freddy told her. 'You've a marvellous voice. Didn't I see you in *Life and Laughter* a few months ago?'

'No, I don't think so. This is my first big part.'

'And it won't be the last, mark my words,' said Trenton enthusiastically.

He was gazing at her with an expression Freddy recognized as one of hopeless devotion, although Desirée seemed not to have noticed it. She smiled at Freddy and said:

'I must just go and change.'

She went away and Freddy asked, 'What was that racket just now?'

'What, the shouting? Oh, it was poor old Rupert. His contract hasn't been renewed and he's taken it badly. Once in a while when he's—I mean to say, once in a while he lets rip at Mr. Gooch and we all have to listen.'

He sat down in front of the glass and touched up his grease-paint, then got up and rummaged in the pockets of an overcoat for some cigarettes.

'Don't you have to change too?' asked Freddy.

'No, I'm done now for the rest of the show. I don't have as many changes as some of the others. Desirée has at least two, I think, and Loveday has several quick changes in the second act and has to do them in the wings.'

'Loveday Curtis?' said Freddy with interest. 'What's she like? I've heard rumours she's difficult to work with.'

Trenton was about to answer when a short, stout man came in. Freddy recognized him as Morry Jinks, one half of the well-known comic double act Jinks and Spooner. Jinks darted Freddy a poisonous glance, gave his balding head a cursory dab with a powder brush in front of the glass, displaced a heap of clothes from an armchair onto the floor then threw himself into it and began leafing through a copy of the *Sporting Times*.

'This is Freddy,' said Trenton. 'He's from the *Clarion*.'

'So?' growled Jinks without looking up.

Freddy, who had been about to offer some friendly remark, decided against it. Trenton made a face and indicated that they should leave the room.

'We're having to share because they've been renovating the dressing-rooms on the other corridor and they're not finished yet,' he said as he shut the door behind him. 'It's a bit of a squeeze. I say, don't you think Jinks's scene with the shark is awfully funny?'

'Rather. He doesn't seem very funny in real life, though.'

'No,' agreed Trenton. 'He has been a bit irritable lately. I find it's better to leave him to himself as much as possible.'

'Is he always like that? And where's Spooner? Don't they usually work together?'

Trenton put a finger over his lips and glanced back at the door.

'Mr. Gooch fired him,' he said in a low voice.

'Who is this Mr. Gooch? He seems to put everybody's back up.'

'Septimus Gooch. The man behind the show. This is his production. He let Spooner go before the start of the run and had his part written out. Jinks wanted to leave too, but his contract wouldn't allow it—I gather he was badly advised when he signed it. Gooch won't let him off, so he's stuck here in this production without his partner until the end of the run. I hear they've missed out on some good opportunities in the meantime.'

'I see. No wonder he's in a foul mood, then,' said Freddy.

A door opened with a clatter just then, and they turned to see a man wearing a magnificent scarlet silk dressing-gown burst out into the corridor, muttering darkly to himself. He caught sight of Freddy and Trenton and jumped slightly. His brow cleared, and Freddy saw a handsome face whose heavy make-up did not quite disguise the lines around the eyes.

'Oh, I thought you were Septimus,' said the man, pronouncing his words very carefully. A faint whiff of whisky hung about him. 'I've just remembered something I forgot to say to him earlier.'

'I don't know where he is,' said Trenton. 'Rupert, this is Freddy Pilkington-Soames. He works for the *Clarion*.'

Rupert removed his right hand from his pocket, looked down at it thoughtfully for a moment, then lifted it as though it did not quite belong to his body.

'Rupert St. Clair,' he said. The handshake was firm enough. He lowered his brow again. 'Well, if he's not here I shall just have to speak to him later.'

He turned with exquisite grace back into his dressing-room, bumping lightly against the door-frame as he did so.

'Does he—' began Freddy, but could not finish his question before a woman's raised voice was heard issuing from a door that stood half-open nearby.

'I won't stand for it!' it cried. 'I can't take it any more. I tell you, I put it on the arm of the sofa last night before I left, so how did it come to be over here on the shelf this afternoon?'

'You ought to know,' returned a rumbling male voice impatiently. 'You must have moved it.'

'I didn't! I remember distinctly I put it here because I was going to read it today when I came in. They promised me a good write-up so I was looking forward to it, but it wasn't where I left it.'

'Well somebody must have done it.'

'But I've asked everybody and nobody did. And it's not the first time, either. It keeps happening. Things being moved when nobody could have moved them. I tell you, it's the ghost!'

'Rubbish! I've told you fifty times there's no ghost.'

'But there is, there is! What else could it be? First the voices and now this. I don't think you care about me at all, Septimus. If you did you wouldn't make me stay in this horrid dressing-room, which I'm certain is haunted. Why can't you put me somewhere else?'

'You know perfectly well there is nowhere else—unless you want to go in with the chorus.'

'I can't go in with them! Why, I'm the star! It wouldn't be right. Besides, they hate me.'

'Well, this is the best we can do. Jenny and Desirée are crammed in together, but you don't hear them complaining.'

The woman's voice went up by perhaps half an octave.

'No, because they're too busy plotting against me! Don't think I don't know what they're up to. Desirée wants my part and Jenny's encouraging her. I've told you to fire them both, so why won't you do it?'

From long experience Freddy recognized the tone of a woman who was building up to a fine explosion of irrational rage. His usual course of action in such a situation would have been to retreat with all due celerity, but the man with the deep voice was evidently made of different stuff.

'Now look here, my girl, we've had this out before. Don't you try that game with me or you'll soon see exactly where you stand. You're getting ideas above your station again.' The voice dropped to a more sinister, meaningful tone. 'Perhaps it's time I moved on after all. Desirée's a nice little piece and she won't give me the same trouble you do.'

Freddy noticed that Trenton had gone puce in the face. The woman in the dressing-room gave a little shriek of rage.

'You don't think I'll stand for that, do you? Why, I'll—I'll kill you first!'

Upon that dramatic exclamation the door was flung wide open and Loveday Curtis appeared. She was blonde and very beautiful, but her pretty face was screwed up into a ball of pink fury. She seemed not to notice Freddy and Trenton as she swept past grandly, calling for her dresser.

'Thaar she blows,' said a voice beside Freddy with some satisfaction. Freddy turned but had no time to register more than a general impression of shining brown curls, a plump mouth painted with red lipstick and an eye-patch, before he suddenly found himself surrounded by a sea of soft flesh, as half a dozen chorus-girls attired in pirate costumes flocked past in a cloud of scent. All coherent thought evaporated from his mind for a moment or two. Then the girl who had spoken passed him again, this time without the eye-patch. Was it the same girl? Freddy craned his neck and tried to pick her out from the milling crowd. No, there she was, wearing an eye-patch, right enough. Freddy blinked and shook his head to clear it.

A man looked out of Loveday Curtis's dressing-room. He was perhaps fifty years of age, a tall and powerful presence with jet-black hair, bushy eyebrows and a high colour.

'Where's Jennings?' he said. 'I want him.'

'Artie, Mr. Gooch wants you,' called one of the chorus-girls.

Septimus, glancing about, spotted Freddy and was about to say something when he saw Alf the stage door-keeper approaching.

'Here, about that—' began Septimus. Alf grimaced, but was saved by the arrival of Artie Jennings, the harassed-looking stage-manager.

'What's that new saxophone player's name?' snapped Septimus. 'Tell him he'll be out of a job if he fluffs that last number one more time.'

'I'll have a word with him,' said Artie, and hurried off. Septimus looked around for Alf, but he had already disappeared. Septimus huffed with impatience and withdrew into Loveday's dressing-room, having seemingly forgotten about Freddy.

'Second act beginners,' came the call, and all at once the confusion and bustle died down and were replaced by a general sense of purpose, as personal concerns were set aside for the good of the show. The theatre was a small one, with dressing-rooms located close to the stage, and the corridor was suddenly full of people. The rest of the chorus came out and shuffled silently out onto the stage. Morry Jinks followed a moment or two later, together with a pleasant-looking woman with large hazel eyes Freddy had not met, but whom he recognized as having played the mother of Loveday and Desirée in the first act.

'I'm not on immediately,' said Trenton. 'You'll stay and watch, won't you? You can take notes and get a different angle for your piece in the paper. Much more interesting than seeing it from the stalls, what?'

'What about this Gooch fellow? Won't he throw me out on my ear?'

'Not if you keep out of his way. I don't know why he's here, as a matter of fact. He doesn't usually come on Saturdays. At any rate, he's all for publicity so I dare say he'll be as sweet as a lamb about it.'

Freddy doubted this, but his interest had been caught by the scenes around him and he had no objection to staying.

'What was that about a ghost, by the way?' he asked.

Trenton was looking about, half-distracted.

'Oh, nothing. We had a little trouble a couple of months ago when a chorus-girl died here, and the rumour went round that she'd been frightened to death by an apparition.'

'Ah yes, I remember the story. So our leading lady thinks the ghost is after her now, does she?'

'Theatre-people are very superstitious,' replied Trenton vaguely. He was still looking around. 'Where's Desirée? She ought to be here by now.'

Freddy followed the performers towards the stage, glancing around for a suitable niche from which to watch proceedings. Septimus Gooch emerged once again from Loveday's dressing-room and Freddy hurriedly retreated behind a length of heavy black curtain. Septimus was not looking for him, however, for he had button-holed Alf the stage door-keeper and they were conferring together about something.

Alf sauntered off and Septimus withdrew into Loveday's room, shutting the door.

The music struck up and the curtain rose and the second act began. Freddy watched as Morry Jinks went into his big comic number with Jenny Minter as his foil. In the wings across the other side of the stage he spied Loveday Curtis submitting to the last-minute attentions of her elderly dresser, who would remain there for the whole of the second act, ready to help Loveday with her quick changes. Freddy watched with interest. After the first number Loveday made her entrance. A minute or two later Desirée arrived breathlessly and went to stand next to Trenton in the wings. Shortly afterwards their cue came and they both went on. Freddy glanced behind him to see Alf passing again, muttering to himself. He shuffled out of sight. Trying to keep his presence a secret seemed a hopeless business, however, for he had barely had ten minutes' peace when he was accosted by the harassed-looking stage-manager.

'Damn, I thought you were Rupert. Where the devil has he got to? He's due on any minute.'

From where Freddy stood he could just glimpse the corridor, where Rupert St. Clair could be seen coming out of his room. Artie Jennings hissed and gesticulated urgently to him. Rupert looked up, mimed an expression of dismay and ran into the wings.

'Awfully sorry, Artie,' he murmured distractedly. He dabbed at his forehead with a handkerchief, drew himself up and made his entrance. Freddy watched half-fearfully, but he need not have worried, for Rupert St. Clair was a seasoned professional and had himself wholly in hand. His performance was faultless. Freddy was impressed.

He settled himself to watch the second act, taking good care to keep out of the way of the cast as they moved on and off the stage. Every so often he looked at his watch, but there was plenty of time before he was expected back at the

Calliope. At last the show came to an end and a suitable number of encores were performed. Then the cast took their bows and the curtain came down for the last time, and everybody left the stage with the sound of applause ringing in their ears.

'Not bad, eh?' said Trenton to Freddy. 'I say, do stay and have a drink. A few of us will be going on to a night-club after we've changed.'

It was nearly a quarter past ten. Freddy had no more than a few minutes to get back to the theatre next door and play his part to Lady Featherstone and Mrs. Belcher, but he was always interested in lending his presence to any festivities that might be going on.

'Where are you going? I can't stay now but I might be able to join you later,' he replied, as Loveday's dresser edged past, muttering under her breath and bearing a pile of costumes.

'Oh, just the Katmandu. Rather old hat nowadays, but still good fun.'

'I—' Freddy began, but got no further because just then a loud cry issued from Loveday's room and the dresser came out in a hurry, white in the face. They all turned to look at her.

'It's Mr. Gooch!' she cried. 'He's dead!'

Chapter Three

FOR A SECOND EVERYONE FELL SILENT.

'What?' demanded Rupert St. Clair. 'What the devil do you mean?'

Loveday pushed through the crowd blocking the corridor and stood before her dresser.

'What are you talking about, Alice?'

Alice lifted a trembling hand and indicated the room from whence she had just emerged.

'I just found him, lying in all of a heap. I swear I didn't do anything. Oh, my heart!'

She put a hand to her breast.

'Oh, Lord,' said Rupert suddenly. He disappeared into the room and came out almost immediately.

She's right!' he exclaimed. 'He's dead!'

Loveday took one look through the door, gave a piercing scream and fainted dead away. As Desirée and Trenton rushed to her aid, Freddy wriggled past them to get a look.

Loveday's dressing-room was slightly larger and more plushly furnished than Trenton's, with thick carpet and a comfortable-looking sofa. Freddy looked round, taking in the scene. Vases of flowers rested upon almost every surface, and the scent of gardenias, freesias, lilies and roses filled the air. Against one wall was a heavy oak cabinet, with next to it a rail that bowed under the weight of the costumes hung upon it. To the left of a wash-basin in the corner a tall steamer trunk stood open, seemingly used as a receptacle for other small items of apparel, which spilled out of its drawers. But none of these things could hold the attention for long, for taking up most of the rest of the room was the figure of Septimus Gooch, who lay supine on the floor in front of the oak cabinet, his eyes staring, his lips pulled back from his teeth in a terrible, ghastly grin. He had knocked over a vase of flowers as he fell, and two or three limp anemones lay damply across his right trouser leg. Freddy advanced cautiously towards the motionless figure.

'Stand back! Don't touch him!'

It was Alf, the stage door-keeper, who had pushed his way through the crowd and into the room. He glanced around and kicked the fallen vase out of the way, then prodded Septimus cautiously with his toe. He crouched stiffly and felt for a pulse.

'He's dead, innee,' he said succinctly.

Any one of them could have told him that, but still a little gasp went up.

'But how?' demanded Desirée from the doorway.

'Banged his head on that cabinet, it looks like,' said Alf. 'He must have fallen over.'

'Let me past, everybody. I want to see,' came a voice. Freddy looked up and saw the woman with hazel eyes standing in the doorway, staring at the scene blankly. She came slowly into the room. 'Septimus,' she said, and there was a catch in her throat. She knelt down next to him, then turned her head towards the onlookers. 'Get out. All of you.'

'We must call a doctor,' said Freddy.

'You leave that to us, Jenny,' said Alf kindly. 'Go and have yourself a sit down and a cuppa tea. Must be a shock, even in spite of everything.'

Jenny stood up and turned to see Loveday swaying in the doorway, supported by Desirée. Loveday was wild-eyed and open-mouthed, and evidently working up to an explosion. It came.

'It's the ghost again, I told you!' she shrieked. 'I knew it would happen—first Una, and now Septimus! I told him, but he wouldn't listen! This place is cursed!'

She gave a high, keening wail, then broke into hysterical sobs.

'Be quiet, Loveday!' said Jenny sharply. 'This is no time for scenes. For heaven's sake, somebody get her some brandy. Trenton, go and call a doctor. Now get out, all of you.'

'Better call the police, too,' said Freddy to Trenton's retreating figure. Loveday was borne away, weeping loudly, while Jenny crouched again by the body of Septimus and Freddy looked around, wondering what had happened. The spilt water from the vase of flowers had seeped into the carpet under Septimus's right knee, while a dark streak of what looked like blood was clearly visible on the cabinet. It looked very much as though he had toppled backwards and knocked his head against the corner. He must have fallen with some force for it to have done so much damage. What had caused him to lose his balance so calamitously? Jenny stood up.

'What do we do now?' she said, more to herself than to Freddy.

'We ought to leave him here and lock the door,' he replied.

She looked up as though seeing him for the first time.

'I don't believe we've been introduced.'

'I beg your pardon. Freddy Pilkington-Soames of the *Clarion*.'

'Oh heavens, the press so soon?'

'I was here already,' said Freddy apologetically. 'I'm a pal of Trenton's. My presence is quite accidental.'

'Well, I suppose it can't be helped. My name's Jenny

Minter, and—I expect I'd better tell you before someone else does—I'm Septimus's wife.'

'I say, I'm awfully sorry.'

'Don't be. It's been a tenuous arrangement for years.' She looked down at Septimus and touched his head lightly. 'Poor idiot. I'd better go and change before the doctor gets here. Do we really need the police?'

'They'll want to investigate how the accident happened.'

'I suppose so. Very well, then. Alf, lock the door, will you?'

She went off, leaving Freddy to answer questions from all the people who had crowded into the corridor, dying to know what was going on.

'I'm afraid it's true, right enough,' he replied. 'Mr. Gooch has met with an accident. He's dead.'

'Serve him right if you ask me,' said Morry Jinks, who had already removed his make-up and changed into his street clothes. Several indignant exclamations broke out from members of the chorus. 'Well, don't be hypocrites. Which of us will miss him?' he demanded.

'Loveday,' said one of the chorus-girls. A few people giggled.

'She'll miss the furs and the diamonds,' said another.

'Hush!' exclaimed a third.

'It's the ghost again, it must be!' squealed a girl with fluffy blonde hair.

'Don't be a fool!' snapped a tall girl fiercely. 'Stop yelping, you idiots—I wish you'd all get it into your silly heads that there's no ghost!'

'But you have to admit it's strange all the same, Peggy,' said the girl with the eye-patch Freddy had seen earlier. She was still in costume, but had flipped up the patch above her eye.

'Dreadfully strange!' agreed the girl next to her, and suddenly Freddy understood what had puzzled him earlier, for she was identical in every way to the girl with the eye-patch.

They must surely be twins. The sisters stared at each other, worried, then back at the tall girl they had addressed as Peggy.

'Do you think—' one of them began doubtfully.

'No I don't!' said Peggy. 'And you're nitwits if you do.'

Trenton approached.

'The doctor's on his way, apparently,' he said. 'Are you going to wait, Freddy? He ought to be here in ten minutes or so. Is it too late for you to 'phone the story to the paper?'

Freddy glanced at his watch and was horrified to find that the hands said ten to eleven. *Consider the Ravens* was long finished, and he had been fairly caught out.

'Confound it!' he exclaimed in dismay. 'I have to go. Sorry, old chap!'

He dashed out through the stage door and up the alley to the Calliope, but it was too late: as he had feared, the front of the theatre was already in darkness, and there was no sign of Lady Featherstone and Mrs. Belcher. Freddy swore to himself. Sir Aldridge would be furious with him for having failed at least to see the ladies into a taxi, and what would his editor, Mr. Bickerstaffe, say when he found out that Freddy had not seen the play at all, given that he was supposed to be writing a review for Monday's edition?

Freddy turned the question over in his mind for a minute or two. Perhaps the situation was not as disastrous as he had feared. True, he had failed to present himself after the play, but that might be explained away with a little thought. He was sure he could think of some excuse for his absence then, but aside from that there was no reason why anybody should know he had removed himself from the theatre for the entire evening. With that comforting thought, he decided to return to the Jollity to observe proceedings. At the stage door he found that the police had just arrived and the doctor was expected, and nobody was inclined to let him in. He waited a while, but it soon became clear that Trenton would not be coming out any time soon, so Freddy left his excuses and decided to make his own arrangements. He put the unfortunate events of that evening out of his mind and repaired to the Excelsior Club, where he could be sure of finding people he knew, and finally rolled into bed, rather the worse for wear, at five o'clock.

Chapter Four

FREDDY WAS awoken on Sunday at a time he considered unreasonable by the ringing of the telephone-bell. He answered it groggily. It was Sir Aldridge Featherstone.

'Where the devil were you last night?' he barked.

Freddy was suddenly wide awake and in a panic. He had completely forgotten to think up an excuse for his absence the night before.

'Ah, yes, sir, I was just about to call you,' he said.

'I should think so! M'wife says you were nowhere to be found last night after the play, and that you left her and my sister high and dry.'

'I know—dreadfully sorry about that, sir, but I had quite the little mishap. You see, I was so bowled over by the play—quite the finest thing I've seen in a long time—that when I stood up to applaud and shout "bravo!" at the end, I accidentally inhaled a bullseye I hadn't had the forethought to swallow first, and had to be escorted from the auditorium in a hurry. Naturally, I knew your wife and sister would be waiting for me, and I tried to tell the usher to let Lady Featherstone know I was indisposed, but given the blockage in my airway all I could gasp out was "Feather! Feather!" and I fear they thought I was mad. At any rate, they thumped me so hard on the back that I nearly fainted, and I was fit for nothing for a good half an hour. By the time my ears had stopped ringing and I'd recovered enough to fasten my tie again, the ladies had left the theatre. You will pass on my deepest apologies, won't you? I was terribly disappointed to have missed them both. Do tell Lady F. I've quite come round to her opinion about the hidden meaning behind that little scene in the first act. She'll know the one I'm talking about.'

It was not exactly satisfactory, but for a man who had been woken up at an indecently early hour he felt it was worthy of some credit. Sir Aldridge was inclined to grumble but seemed to accept Freddy's story. Freddy put the receiver down, congratulating himself on having talked his way out of trouble. Now all he had to do was write his review for the paper—he was confident of his ability to invent something convincing, despite having missed the whole play—and nobody would ever know. He felt a pang of regret that he would not be able to boast of getting the scoop on the events at the Jollity, but it was obviously impossible for him to admit that he had been present at the time, so he had no choice but to let that particular opportunity slip through his fingers.

The next week was a busy one, and Freddy quite forgot about *Have At It!* and the strange death of Septimus Gooch until Friday morning, when Trenton Bagshawe turned up at the offices of the *Clarion.*

'I'm on my way to the inquest, and I thought I'd look in to see if you were coming,' he said.

Freddy was wrestling with phraseology in an attempt to stretch a three hundred-word story into a seven hundred-word space, and stared at Trenton blankly.

'The inquest?'

'Mr. Gooch. I expect all the theatre press will be there, but I thought it might make the general newspapers too. You'll come, won't you? We might go for lunch afterwards.'

Freddy saw with alarm that his editor, Mr. Bickerstaffe, was standing only two desks away. Freddy put a finger over his lips and shook his head urgently at Trenton, but it was too late.

'What's this?' demanded Mr. Bickerstaffe.

'I beg your pardon, sir,' said Trenton. 'I just wanted to know whether Freddy was coming to report on the inquest into Septimus Gooch's death, since he was there on the spot, so to speak. It was last Saturday night,' he added helpfully.

Freddy held his breath, hoping against hope that his editor would not put two and two together. Bickerstaffe frowned.

'Last Saturday? But weren't you at the Max D'Auberville play with Lady Featherstone?'

'Oh no, sir,' said Trenton happily. 'Freddy came to see my show, *Have At It!* that night, and was there when Mr. Gooch died.'

'No I wasn't,' said Freddy, resorting desperately to a flat denial. 'You must be thinking of someone else.'

Trenton did not take the hint.

'Of course I'm not. It was you, all right. Don't tell me you don't remember! You turned up at the interval then watched the second act from the wings, and then when Mr. Gooch died you went into the room and looked around and told me to call the police. Surely you can't have forgotten already!'

Mr. Bickerstaffe had by now attained a state of enlightenment. He drew himself up.

'Am I to understand you weren't there at all that night?' he growled. 'Sir Aldridge told me some story about how you'd disappeared into thin air. Do you mean to say you reviewed *Consider the Ravens* without even seeing it?'

'Not at all, sir. As a matter of fact I'd seen it twice already before then,' lied Freddy. 'Quite a marvellous piece. Full of depth and feeling, with a moral message that oughtn't to be ignored, just as I said in my review.'

There was a menacing look in Bickerstaffe's eye.

'Is that so? It sounds just up my street. I've a mind to see it myself. Give me a summary of the plot, won't you? Jolliffe will tell me if it's right,' he said, turning his attention to the young man sitting at the next desk to Freddy. 'You've seen it, I expect, haven't you, Jolliffe?'

'Yes, sir,' said Jolliffe smugly. Freddy threw him a glare and reached for his jacket.

'I'd be delighted, but I'd better get going if I'm to make the inquest. We don't want to miss this story, do we? I'll tell you all about the play this afternoon. Come on, Trenton, or we'll be late.'

Before Bickerstaffe could protest he had already clapped his hat on his head and was halfway out of the office. Trenton scurried after him.

'I say, old chap, I haven't got you into trouble, have I?' he said as they came out into the street.

Freddy gave a hollow laugh, but had no time to reply for a bus was just passing and they had to run to catch it. They arrived at the coroner's court and found seats at the back. Loveday Curtis, Rupert St. Clair and Jenny Minter had already arrived and were sitting at the front. Freddy glanced around. A little way away, the chorus-girl called Peggy and the twins were whispering together with a fourth girl. There was no sign of Morry Jinks.

The inquest began and the facts of the matter were stated baldly. Shorn of the agitation and the noise of the theatre that night, it was a plain, ordinary tale. A man had stumbled backwards and caught his head on the edge of a wooden cabinet, which had killed him almost instantly. Those who had witnessed the events of that evening were called to speak, but nobody was able to shed much light on the matter. Even the exact time of death was unknown: all that could be said with any certainty was that Septimus Gooch had been alive at the beginning of the second act and dead by the end of it.

A dry medical man then affirmed that he had found no

trace of heart disease in the deceased or any other condition that might have caused him to fall in such a manner, nor was there any suggestion that he had ever suffered from fainting fits. In the absence of any other evidence, it was the medical man's opinion that Septimus Gooch had lost his balance for some unknown reason, fallen and knocked his head upon the wooden cabinet.

At last, the coroner announced that there was no way of knowing what had caused the deceased to fall, but since there were no suspicious circumstances he had no hesitation in recording a verdict of accidental death.

Everyone filed out and Trenton said:

'Where shall we go for lunch? Half a mo, I must just say something to Rupert.'

He disappeared, and Freddy took the opportunity to scribble down a few notes. When he looked up he found Jenny Minter standing before him. She seemed a little agitated.

'I want to speak to you,' she said. 'But not here and now. Where can we talk?'

'Would you like me to come to the theatre later?'

'Perhaps better not, as I'd rather not be overheard.' She thought a moment. 'Suppose you meet me outside the Piccadilly Corner House at five.'

'Very well,' agreed Freddy and she went off. He watched her go, wondering what it was all about.

He spent the afternoon trying to avoid Mr. Bickerstaffe and was a few minutes late for the meeting, but he found that Jenny had only just arrived herself.

'I thought we might walk, but I'd forgotten it would be dark by now,' she said. The early evening air was cold and damp and the lights of the Corner House shone out invitingly into the street. 'Shall we go inside? It doesn't look too busy.'

They did so and a smartly dressed nippy took their order.

'I've been talking to Susan Browncliffe,' said Jenny, once the tea had arrived.

'Susan—oh, you mean Lady Browncliffe? Is she a friend of yours?'

'Yes, we were at school together. She says you did first-rate work in the Westray case, and solved the whole thing when everybody including the police thought it was suicide. You were quite marvellous, she said.'

'Oh, I say, what?' said Freddy modestly.

'But you're not a detective, are you?'

'No, just a common or garden newspaper reporter, I'm afraid. Why?'

She sipped her tea, seeming to consider.

'You were at the Jollity on Saturday,' she said at last. 'You saw what happened. Do you believe Septimus's death was an accident?'

Freddy raised his eyebrows.

'Well, that's what the inquest concluded, and I've no reason to think otherwise. It certainly looked accidental. Why? Don't you?'

'No.'

'Why not?'

She hesitated.

'I don't quite know. You're right—it did look perfectly accidental, but it's just wrong, somehow, in a way I can't put my finger on, except to say that Septimus was the toughest, healthiest, most *vital* person I've ever known. The idea of him losing his balance for no good reason and hitting his head makes no sense at all. If he'd had a heart problem or some-thing like that, then I might have understood it, but he didn't, and they didn't find anything else wrong with him either. Of course you might say I'm shocked and can't think straight, and if it had just been Septimus I dare say I'd have accepted the verdict and tried to forget about it. But his isn't the first death, you see—someone else died in very similar circumstances a couple of months ago.'

'Ah yes, a chorus-girl, wasn't it?'

'Yes. Una Bryant, her name was. She was only seventeen or eighteen. It was very sad.'

'What happened there, exactly?'

'She was found dead in her dressing-room after the performance, but they don't really know how she died. It can't possibly be a coincidence, can it? Two deaths from unknown causes in as many months is too much to swallow.'

'I've seen stranger things,' said Freddy. 'You'd be surprised.'

'Perhaps, but I don't like it. I've been feeling uncomfortable about it all week and wondering whether to mention it to someone, but everybody else seems blithely unsuspicious of anything untoward, so I kept quiet. And then Susan Browncliffe happened to mention you, and I thought perhaps you might be curious enough about it to look into it for me.'

'It's not quite true that nobody else thinks there's anything odd about what happened, though, is it? Wasn't there some story about the theatre's being haunted? As I understand, half the cast of *Have At It!* believe there's a spectral hand behind all this, smiting down theatre-folk right and left as it wafts its ghostly presence through the theatre.'

'Oh, nonsense. It was Loveday who started that. Nobody would have thought a thing about it if it hadn't been for her.'

'But why did the story start? Who is this ghost meant to be?'

'The Jollity as it stands today is fairly new. The old theatre burned to the ground about twenty-five years ago and the story goes that someone died in the fire and their spirit now haunts the new building—although I can tell you for a fact that's not true, since I was there at the time and remember it all perfectly well. One person was injured, but nobody died. It was shortly before our marriage, and the Jollity was Septimus's first theatre, and the one that made his fortune once it had been rebuilt. Recently they've had to make some alterations to accommodate the modern type of show, and the plumbing also needed fixing in some of the dressing-rooms, so we're all crammed together into one corridor at the moment. Loveday didn't like that and made a fuss. Then she heard the old ghost story and started imagining she could hear voices in her dressing-room just because she wanted to be moved somewhere else. After that Una died and half the chorus took up the cry and Septimus had to be quite firm with them to stop them talking about it.'

'Don't you believe in ghosts yourself?' asked Freddy.

'Of course I do. I'm as superstitious as the next actress, but whoever heard of a ghost frightening anybody—two people, in fact—literally to death? I might possibly have believed it of Una, but any ghost would have had no luck trying anything of the kind with Septimus, since he simply didn't believe in them. He hadn't any imagination at all. That's why he was so successful in the business—he saw everything in terms of pounds, shillings and pence.'

'Then what do you think happened?'

'I don't know. As I said, he could be difficult at times, and he'd rubbed a lot of people up the wrong way lately. He was what I'd call a steam-roller—if he saw you as an obstacle then he'd simply roll over you and crush you. I don't think he meant to be bad, but he'd worked hard for his success and he'd forgotten what it was like to be an ordinary person. It simply never occurred to him that he couldn't have whatever he wanted.'

'Do you think somebody killed him deliberately?'

'Oh dear, it does sound rather blunt when you put it like that. But there's no denying he did have plenty of enemies.'

'People who disliked him enough to murder him?'

'Perhaps. I don't know.'

'In that case where does Una Bryant come into it? Who wanted her dead?'

'Nobody, as far as I can see. She wasn't unpopular—far

from it, in fact. I know several of the chorus were quite cut up about her death.'

'But if you're right, and the fact of there having been two deaths means something suspicious has been going on, then they must be connected, don't you see?'

'Yes, I do.'

'It's all very vague,' said Freddy. 'I'm not sure what you expect me to do about it.'

'I'm not sure myself. Perhaps I just wanted someone to talk to. At least you haven't laughed at me.'

'No, I'd never do that, but to be quite frank you haven't told me anything to convince me there's anything untoward about the two deaths, except to say you think your husband was too steady on his feet to fall over. Do you have any idea of what might have killed him, if not that?'

'Not really. If anything I suppose I'd got it into my head that someone had a row with him, hit him and knocked him over.'

'I can think of two arguments against that: one, Septimus was a hefty chap, and it would take another hefty chap to take him out, and two, surely someone would have heard if there'd been a rumpus of that kind going on? I'd have heard it myself, as a matter of fact, since I was standing in the wings during the second half of the performance.'

'Not necessarily,' she replied. 'The music and singing might easily have drowned any sound out. Several of the numbers in the second act are very loud and lively.'

'True,' admitted Freddy. 'My first point still stands, though. I'm not sure anything I can do will unearth the real story—if there *is* a real story. But there's another good reason to leave well alone—perhaps the most important one of all. Looking into this would mean investigating people who are perhaps your friends. You'd have to give me names and motives. Wouldn't it be better to leave well alone? Nobody will think the worse of you for it, since nobody has the slightest inkling that there might have been anything fishy about Septimus's death. I'm not convinced there was myself, and I don't want to go in there and stir up a hornets' nest for nothing.'

'I hadn't thought of it like that.' She sighed. 'You're right, of course. I don't see how you could find out how Una or Septimus died if the doctors and the police don't know, and it's not fair to go around upsetting people for nothing. Forget I asked, then. It was silly of me, and I hadn't thought it through.'

She stirred her tea and they sat in silence for a few moments. Freddy regarded Jenny, who looked unhappy.

'Oh, very well,' he said suddenly. 'It can't do any harm to do a little digging, although I don't expect I shall find anything very much.'

She brightened.

'You'll do it? Oh, thank you! There's no need to spend too much time on it, only Susan said you were awfully good at spotting things other people wouldn't notice. If you don't find anything out after a day or two then we'll leave it there and no harm done.'

'How can I do it, though? I can't just barge into the theatre asking people if they were responsible for old Septimus's getting a crack on the coconut. What shall I say?'

Jenny thought.

'I know—let's say you're writing a piece about Septimus's life for your paper. I'll tell everyone I've given you permission to ask them questions. I expect most of them will be only too pleased to talk to you, although you'll have to expect them to talk about themselves mainly.'

'Who inherits his business, by the way?' asked Freddy, struck by the easy way in which she talked about giving permission.

'As far as I know I do. Septimus didn't trust people in general, but he knew I'd a head for business and always said he'd leave it all to me.'

'Then you're a suspect, too,' said Freddy lightly.

'Am I? But why would I bring you into it if I'd done it? It would make far more sense to leave well alone.'

'True. Very well, we'll leave you out of it for the present. So, then, tell me which of the cast and all the other people running around the Jollity had a good reason to want your husband dead.' He took out his notebook. 'I'll make a list. I know of two already: Rupert St. Clair, who didn't have a contract but wanted one, and Morry Jinks, who had a contract but didn't want it.' He paused delicately. 'What about Miss Curtis?'

'Loveday? What do you mean?'

'Weren't they…?'

'Oh, that. Yes, they were, but it wasn't very serious on Septimus's part. After we separated there was always a young thing tagging along, but they all seemed to merge into one another after a while. Loveday was just the latest. But yes, I see what you mean. I suppose you could say she had a motive. She'd got it into her head that he was going to marry her, and didn't take it well when he said he had no intention of doing anything of the sort. I felt sorry for her, to tell the truth. She's quite a new star, you know, and she's certainly a talent, but I don't know that she has what it takes to last the distance. I think she was unsure of her standing with Septimus, and rightly so. He would have moved on to someone else sooner or later.'

Freddy made a note.

'Who else? Trenton. He's my pal so obviously I don't want to think badly of him, but they're all cracked in his family. His brother St. John is a revolutionary Communist who spends half his time thinking up ever more imaginative ways to over-throw the Government, so I shouldn't be a bit surprised to hear Trenton had had some kind of brain-storm and decided society needed to be rid of all theatre producers with black hair, or something of the kind.'

Jenny said kindly:

'Trenton is a dear and hadn't fallen out with Septimus as far as I know. I can't think of any reason why he would have killed him.'

'What about Desirée?'

She hesitated.

'I told you—you can't pick and choose your potential killers,' said Freddy. 'There's no use in your trying to shield people if you want the truth.'

'Of course you're right, it's just she's a sweet girl. Rather an innocent, but there's been talk.'

'Of what?'

'I told you Septimus would move on from Loveday one day. Well…' she made an expressive face.

'You think Desirée had him in her sights?'

'No, quite the opposite. He'd been pursuing her and she wasn't interested. But as I said, Septimus liked to get his own way. She was unhappy about it, and I'd been meaning to have a word with him and tell him to leave her alone, but I didn't get the chance.'

'Hmm. I can see how that might lead to a scene, although I can't picture Desirée laying Septimus out with a well-placed left hook to the jaw. But you see, this brings Trenton back into the thing.'

'Does it?'

'Yes. I don't know if you've noticed, but he's goopy about her. Perhaps he was feeling all protective-like, and decided to take matters into his own hands.'

'Oh, surely not! I can't see Trenton as a murderer.'

'There's nothing to say it was intentional. If someone did decide to have a go at Septimus, they may not have intended to kill him, but once he went down and was clearly dead, whoever it was would have to make himself scarce pretty quick.'

'I suppose so.' She looked a little distressed. 'You're right—

it's not much fun when there's a chance somebody one likes might have done it.'

'It isn't, is it? Let's hope they didn't, then. Now, is that everybody? Any of the musicians or the chorus?'

Jenny thought.

'Any one of the musicians might have *wanted* to do it, but none of them could have since they were all in the pit throughout the second act. And I don't see how any of the chorus could have knocked him over. Most of them are tiny.'

'The same goes for all the ladies, I should say. What about the stage-manager—what's his name? Artie Jennings?'

'He and Septimus got along well mostly, so I don't know why he'd want to kill him.'

'Well, I can tell you about Artie Jennings, because I had him in sight and could see him for pretty much the whole of the second act, standing in the prompt corner. He came looking for Rupert at one point but then returned to his station. Very well, this lot will do to be going on with. There are plenty of people with a motive, but not all of them had an opportunity. What are you hoping I'll find out, by the way? I mean to say, would it make you happier if I found out Septimus's death *was* the result of nefarious doings?'

'No,' she replied. 'But it might settle my mind.'

They parted soon afterwards, Freddy having agreed to come to the Jollity as soon as he could and start his inquiry. It was only a little after six, and since he had nothing arranged for that evening he went with some reluctance to see *Consider the Ravens*, just in case Mr. Bickerstaffe remembered his threat to examine him on the plot. It was every bit as dull as he had expected—so much so that he fell asleep in the middle of the first act and had to go and see it again the next day.

Chapter Five

IT WAS ALL VERY WELL HAVING PROMISED to investigate the death of Septimus Gooch, but where was Freddy to begin? It seemed an impossible task, but he had agreed to do it, so he spent some time on Saturday writing down what he remembered of the evening in question. It occurred to Freddy that if there had been foul play then he was an important witness, having been present and more or less within sight of the door of Loveday Curtis's dressing-room throughout the second act of the performance. It was only a pity that his attention had been mostly taken up with watching the show, so whoever it was (if there were indeed such a 'whoever') might easily have slipped in and done whatever it was (and what *was* it, exactly?) while Freddy's back was turned.

Leaving aside the question of how someone might have knocked a solidly-built man of six foot three backwards with enough force to crack his skull, if Septimus *had* been killed deliberately, then who had had the opportunity to do it? According to the inquest, Septimus Gooch had died some time between the beginning of act two at five past nine and the end of the performance at just after ten. Assuming it was one of the actors, which of them had come offstage during the second act for long enough to do the deed? Freddy cast his mind back. His memories of the show were a little hazy, but as far as he could recall, all of them—Loveday, Rupert, Desirée, Trenton, Morry Jinks and Jenny herself—had come offstage at one time or another, variously waiting by the stage for their next entrance or running back to their rooms to change. What of the backstage workers? Artie Jennings the stage-manager had been mostly in Freddy's view, standing in the prompt corner when he was not looking about for missing actors, while Alf had supposedly been manning the stage door, although Freddy recalled he had deserted his post several times to come and watch the show. Of the various stage-hands and scenery operators he had seen, all had appeared wholly occupied with their jobs. It was possible, he supposed, that one of them might have absented himself long enough to commit a murder. The stage door-keeper's box had a partial view of the corridor, and Freddy made a note to ask Alf whether he had seen anything suspicious during those moments when he had been where he was meant to be. The only other suspect Freddy could think of was the hapless saxophone player who had been threatened with the sack, but as Jenny had already pointed out, it would certainly have caused comment had he wandered off during the performance to confront his employer. Freddy regarded his notebook in dissatisfaction, with the increasing suspicion that he was about to be drawn into a wild-goose chase that would only be a waste of every-body's time.

He was still pondering the case on Saturday evening while dining out with Gertie. She chided him more than once for his distraction, but he could not prevent his mind from drifting back to the events of a week ago.

'What did I just say?' said Gertie, after he had failed to respond to several of her remarks.

'Eh? What's that?' Something in her tone made him look

up. There was a dangerous glint in her eye. This was a test. Freddy cast about desperately.

'You said your mother wants me to come to dinner next Thursday?' he hazarded.

'I said that ten minutes ago. Since then I've talked about the picnic at Hampton Court last August, Clemmie's tedious scholarly paper on electrified particles, and how much we all laughed the other week when Mungo shot that pheasant and it fell on his head. Why aren't you listening? Don't tell me it's because I'm dull and lacking in conversation, because I happen to know I'm tremendously interesting and fascinating.'

Freddy pulled himself together.

'Sorry, old girl, I'm a little distracted this evening. I had an odd request this week, and it's perplexing me rather.'

'Oh? What sort of odd request?'

'I've been asked to investigate a murder—although I'm not in the least certain it *is* a murder. I was at the Jollity Theatre last week when the producer of the show fell and hit his head in the dressing-room of the leading lady, who happens to be his current inamorata. The inquest said it was an accident and I can't see how anybody could possibly have killed him if it was deliberate.'

'Well, then, it's quite obvious it *wasn't* murder, isn't it?' said Gertie.

Put like that, it seemed very simple. She was probably right. Freddy shook himself mentally and set himself to be entertaining, and the rest of the evening went more smoothly.

On Monday he went to the stage door of the Jollity before the evening performance as promised, and was admitted without difficulty. He found Trenton alone in his dressing-room, occupied with make-up.

'Jenny says you're going to write an obituary for Mr. Gooch, and we're to answer any questions you have,' said Trenton. 'What sort of thing do you want to know?'

'Anything you can think of, really,' replied Freddy. 'I'm

looking for some details of his last moments and what-not. You know, what he said to you before you went onstage, and how you had no notion it would be the last time you'd ever speak to him before the light in his eyes dimmed forever, that sort of stuff. Anything to get the readers weeping uncontrollably into their Lapsang Souchong. Obviously I've my own memories of the thing, but it'll be all the better if I can get some of your thoughts as to what happened in his final moments.'

'Why, I couldn't tell you, old chap. I think the last words he spoke to me were "Fasten your tie properly, Bagshawe." Not exactly poignant, is it?'

'Not exactly,' agreed Freddy. 'When did he say that?'

'Oh, before the first act.'

'And when was the last time you saw him?'

'When you did, I expect. We were all in the corridor and he was bellowing something about the sax player, don't you remember?'

'And you didn't see him after that? You didn't come back to your room during the second half and see him then?'

'No, there isn't time for that. I come off two or three times, but only for a minute or two, and when I'm off I stand stage right waiting for my cue. I don't have any changes in the second act.'

'Stage right? That's the opposite side of the stage from the dressing-rooms, isn't it? What about Desirée, then? Perhaps she saw him. You said she has several changes—does she come back to her dressing-room? Hers is the room nearest the stage, isn't it?'

'Yes, she's in with Jenny. Desirée does come back for her changes, but she doesn't have more than three or four minutes to do it and get back on. I doubt she stopped to talk to Mr. Gooch.' He lowered his voice. 'She wasn't especially keen on him, to be perfectly honest.'

'Why not?'

Trenton flushed.

'He wasn't the thing, that's all. He certainly wasn't a gentleman.'

'I see—the pestering sort, was he?'

'Yes, and she didn't like it. Desirée is a *nice* girl. At any rate, we're awfully pleased that Jenny is in charge of things for the present.'

'She is, is she? I wondered how the show would get along without its producer.'

'It can get along without him easily enough—for a while, at least. Jenny told us this morning that Mr. Gooch left everything to her, and we're all to answer to her for the time being until she's spoken to the lawyers and the money-men and decided what to do about everything. *Have At It!* is meant to be touring the provinces in the new year, and there are still lots of things to settle about that.'

'Whether it will still go ahead, for one, I imagine,' said Freddy.

'Oh, it's quite decided, but I expect some things will have to be rearranged or renegotiated. I don't know how it all works.'

'Shall you be staying with the company?'

'Yes, I signed my contract a few weeks ago.'

'What about Desirée?'

'I don't know. She wasn't sure whether she wanted to, what with the way Gooch was going on, but everything's changed now, hasn't it?' Trenton brightened. 'I must just have a word with her. Perhaps that hasn't occurred to her yet.'

He stood up just as Morry Jinks came in, whistling.

'Evening, evening!' said Jinks genially. 'And how are we all today?'

The contrast between his present demeanour and that which he had displayed on the night of Septimus Gooch's death could not have been starker.

'Hallo, Jinks. Freddy's here to write a piece about Mr. Gooch,' said Trenton.

Jinks twisted his mouth briefly.

'Well, don't ask me for the old black tie stuff. Far as I'm concerned, it's good riddance. He was a vicious old brute who did nothing but make all our lives a misery. High time he got his just deserts if you ask me.'

'I say, I shouldn't go that far,' objected Trenton.

'That's 'cause you hadn't known him long enough. Mark my words, he'd have ground you down too in the end,' said Jinks darkly. He turned to Freddy. 'Anyway, if you want the full water-works, have a word with her next door.'

'Loveday, do you mean?' asked Freddy.

'That's her. She'll do you proud. Just make sure you take it all with fifty pinches of salt.'

With that admonition, he sat down before the glass and began rooting through the boxes and jars on the dressing-table. Trenton went out, presumably in search of Desirée, and Freddy said to Jinks:

'Odd sort of way to die, wasn't it? How do you think it happened? Did you see or hear anything?'

'I was onstage for most of the second act, my boy—didn't notice a thing,' replied Jinks cheerfully.

'Don't you come off to change?'

'Just once—a quick dash to the dressing-room then back, at the same time as Jenny.'

This was true as far as Freddy could remember from having watched the show.

'And you didn't speak to Septimus or see him at all?'

'Never clapped eyes on him, and I wouldn't have spoken to him if I had.'

'Then you haven't had any thoughts as to how he died so suddenly like that?'

'Don't know and don't care. If you ask me he'd had one over the eight and tripped over his own feet.'

'Was he a drinker? The inquest didn't mention anything of the sort.'

Jinks shrugged but made no reply.

'I heard you'd been wanting to leave the show and Septimus wasn't keen on letting you go,' Freddy pursued. 'I suppose his death has been fortunate for you in a way.'

'That's right,' answered Jinks. 'I've had a word with Jenny and she's as good as said we can be off in a couple of weeks.'

'We?'

'I, I meant. When you've been in a double act for as long as I have you get into the way of talking for both of you.'

Freddy asked one or two more questions, but the comedian clearly had no interest in talking about the circumstances of Septimus's death, so Freddy gave it up. He went out and was just about to knock on the door of Loveday Curtis's room when he saw Loveday herself just arriving through the stage door, wearing an expensive-looking fur coat and carrying a bouquet of flowers.

'People will insist on asking for autographs and making one late,' she said, sweeping grandly into her dressing-room and tossing the bouquet carelessly onto the sofa. Looking Freddy up and down, she said, 'You're the press-man, aren't you? Would you be a darling and put those in some water for me?'

There was an empty vase resting on a radiator by the wash-basin, and Freddy obliged as Loveday threw off her fur and examined her reflection in the glass.

'I can barely face going on,' she said. 'But one can't disappoint one's fans, can one?'

'You were very upset by Septimus's death, then?' asked Freddy.

'Yes, I—' Her face crumpled and she sat down suddenly on the sofa, put her hands to her eyes and began to weep elegantly. After a minute or two she took a deep breath and raised a face to him that spoke of unspeakable tragedy courageously borne. 'I'm sorry, I didn't mean to break down like that. I'm afraid I haven't slept a wink in days. To be perfectly honest, I don't know whether I'll ever get over it.'

Whether she were sincere or not it was very well done, Freddy had to admit.

'I've thought time and time again that if only I'd come back to my room during the second act instead of getting changed in the wings I might have been able to save him somehow. But there wasn't the time. And now I have to come here every day and be reminded of it. It's too much! How can one be expected to *work* in these conditions? You wouldn't think I was the star, would you? They say we're only in these rooms because they can't find anywhere else to put us while the works are going on, although they ought to have been finished months ago. I don't see why I couldn't have had one of the bigger rooms but they've put the chorus into those.'

'Well there are quite a few girls and they wouldn't all fit into this small one,' said Freddy reasonably.

She sniffed as though in disagreement, but did not argue. Instead, she said:

'Jenny said you're writing an obituary or something. It's just like her not to think of other people's feelings. "I can't possibly talk about Septimus," I told her. "How could you ask me to do it?"'

'I do beg your pardon, I wouldn't dream of pressing you for a quote if you're too upset,' said Freddy. 'I'll go if you like.'

He would have bet a pound to a penny that she would not want him to leave, and he was right.

'No, there's no need,' she said bravely. 'I hope I know what's due to Septimus. What is it you want me to tell you? I suppose you know that he and I were to be married— although perhaps you don't, since Jenny certainly won't have mentioned it.'

'I had heard something of the kind,' he replied. 'That's why I wanted to speak to you in particular. You more than anyone else must be able to tell me how Septimus spent his final hours. You were one of the last people to speak to him during the interval, I believe?'

She gave a little sob.

'Yes, I was, but I can't tell you much about what we said—just the usual sort of nonsense people in love say to one another, you know.'

'Was that before or after you had the row with him?' asked Freddy innocently.

Loveday's mask slipped for the merest second and she looked furious, but quickly recovered herself.

'That wasn't a row,' she said. 'Not a proper one, at least. Strange things have been happening recently, and I've been rattled, so I got a little heated, that's all.'

'What sort of strange things?'

'Why, this theatre is haunted, and I've been the one to suffer from it. I have the temperament of an artiste, you see, and I'm very sensitive to atmosphere. Not everybody is susceptible to these sorts of influences, but I am, and Septimus didn't understand that.'

'Influences? What do you mean by that, exactly?'

'Well, it started with ghostly, disembodied voices, whispering things.'

'What kind of things?'

She went slightly pink.

'Oh, personal matters. Facts about me that I prefer to keep private. And they accused me of horrid things that weren't true. It was quite upsetting.'

'They? Was there more than one voice?'

'Yes, there were several.'

'Male or female?'

'I don't know. I couldn't tell, but I think perhaps both. Sometimes there was a voice that was a kind of high-pitched hiss, and other times there was a much lower one—a growling sort of sound. There were other ones too, but I was too frightened to pay much attention.'

'And where did you hear them?'

'Here, in this room,' she said, glancing around fearfully as though she expected them to start up again at any moment.

'Anywhere else, or just here?'

'No, just here.'

Freddy gazed around the room. It seemed an odd sort of place for a haunting, being small and cluttered, with people presumably coming in and out all the time.

'Did anyone else hear anything?' he asked.

'No, only me, as far as I know.'

'Was anybody here with you when the voices were speaking, or did they come only when you were alone?'

'Only when I was alone. Once or twice when it happened I ran out and got someone to come in and hear them, but by that time they'd always stopped. It was terribly frustrating, because that made it seem as though I was imagining things, but I most certainly wasn't.'

She glared at him as though daring him to contradict her.

'Do the voices come often?' asked Freddy. 'When was the last time you heard them?'

'As a matter of fact, I don't think I've heard them in weeks. How strange! Oh, yes, I remember now—I'd been hearing them all the time, and was starting to think I should go quite mad, and then Una died, and I just *knew* it was because of the ghost as I'd heard the voices not an hour earlier. But I don't believe I've heard anything since then. Poor Una,' she said, almost as an afterthought.

'That's good news, surely? Perhaps the ghost has gone away.'

'But that's just what it hasn't done! It's still here, I know it. The voices might have stopped, but now it's trying to frighten me in other ways. My things are being moved around—nothing important, just little things, but very noticeable all the same. I left a pair of shoes here by the sofa a couple of weeks ago, for example, and when I came back I found them put over here in the corner. And then the night Septimus died there was a magazine I'd left just here, meaning to read it the next day, but it had been moved. And there have been lots of other little things like that, just as though someone had been in the dressing-room.'

'But what makes you think it was a ghost? Surely anyone here might have done those things?'

'No!' she said triumphantly. 'Not at all. I'm most particular about locking the door when I leave the theatre. I give the keys to Alf, who keeps them in his cabinet. He says nobody could possibly have got them. So you see, it must be a ghost! Besides, other people have noticed it too. Several of the chorus found their things were being moved around, and I heard one of the girls saw a ghostly figure drifting around the theatre late one night—although I couldn't tell you anything much about that, since they won't speak to—that is, I don't have a lot of time to speak to them. At any rate, I'd just started to think I was safe because the voices had stopped, but then when this all started I realized I wasn't safe at all, and the ghost was coming for me next. But it didn't—it got Septimus instead. I'm sure it was a mistake. It meant to get me, but Septimus happened to be there and...'

She made an expressive gesture.

'What do you think the ghost did, exactly?' asked Freddy.

'Why, frightened him to death, of course, just as it did Una,' she replied. 'What other explanation is there?'

'I've no idea,' said Freddy.

Chapter Six

FREDDY CAME out of Loveday's room, musing over what he had just heard. The moving of the shoes and the magazine might easily be explained by absent-mindedness—her own or someone else's—but the story of the voices was a strange one, right enough. Although several people had reported their things having been moved, however, nobody other than Loveday had heard the voices, and since Freddy judged Loveday to be the type of woman who could not do without having everyone's attention upon her, he was inclined to follow Morry Jinks's advice to take everything she said with a pinch of salt. It was possible she had not invented the story entirely, but he had no doubt she was the sort to take a minor occurrence and exaggerate it out of all proportion. Freddy guessed she had overheard people talking about her—after all, the dressing-rooms were packed close together and it was likely that conversations carried through the walls—and had worked it up into a tale of a supernatural presence. Whether any of this were relevant to the death of Septimus Gooch was doubtful, however.

He was pondering what to do next when a door behind him was flung open and a young woman in pronounced dishabille came out, ran down the corridor, burst into another room and emerged again immediately, chattering brightly to another young woman who was even more incompletely clothed than the first, if possible. It was the twins. They stopped dead when they saw Freddy and eyed him with interest. Neither of them seemed in the least troubled about their state of undress. One of them had an unlit cigarette dangling from the corner of her mouth, which was the only way he could tell them apart.

'Got a light?' she said.

Freddy obliged.

'You haven't seen anything of this ghost, have you?' he inquired of them.

'What? Oh, you've been talking to Loveday, I suppose,' said the twin with the cigarette.

'Yes. She says someone has been moving your things about.'

She looked at her sister. 'Not mine, but Maudie's had a silk scarf go missing, haven't you?'

Maudie nodded.

'Miss Curtis also mentioned hearing voices,' said Freddy.

The twins giggled.

'She's got a screw loose if you ask me,' replied Maudie. 'She dragged Minnie into her dressing-room one night and said a ghost was whispering to her, but you didn't hear a thing, did you, Minnie?'

'Not a thing,' agreed Minnie.

'What about your friends in the chorus? Did any of them hear anything?'

'Hmph,' said Maudie. 'Some of them *said* they did at first. When Loveday started making a fuss a few of them started claiming they could hear ghostly noises too, but then Peggy pointed out it was just the water pipes clanking and they had to shut up.' She snorted. 'Some people will believe anything.'

'Then you don't think the voices existed?'

''Course not. I reckon Loveday was making it up. She's never happy unless she's the centre of attention.'

Since this was exactly the conclusion that Freddy had reached, he let that particular question drop.

'And what about—er—ghostly presences? Anything of that sort?'

'We haven't seen anything,' they replied, shaking their heads in unison.

'Why do you want to know?' asked Maudie curiously.

'I'm at the *Clarion*. I've come to write a piece about Septimus Gooch.'

'Old Hoochie-Goochie? Nasty accident, that was.'

'It was,' agreed Freddy. 'Queer sort of thing to happen. Miss Curtis believes he was frightened to death, but I suppose you think that's nonsense.'

'Well—' began Minnie.

'Of course it is,' said Maudie at the same time.

'Odd, coming so soon after another death,' observed Freddy. 'Wasn't there a girl who died here not long ago too? Una Bryant, I believe her name was. Was she a friend of yours?'

They exchanged glances then gave him identical sideways looks. The effect was most disconcerting.

'Una? Yes she was,' said Maudie.

Freddy was about to ask another question when the door by which they were standing opened and the girl called Peggy came out in full costume and make-up.

'What are you two chattering about?' she said. 'You'd better get ready or Artie will give you what for.'

She gave Freddy an assessing look, eyes narrowed, then turned back into the room.

'Oh Lord!' exclaimed Minnie. 'We're going to be late. We'd better go. What's your name, by the way?'

'Freddy,' said Freddy.

'Well, Freddy, maybe we'll see you later.'

On that promise they both winked at him and disappeared into the dressing-room, arm in arm. Freddy straightened his tie.

'Act One beginners please,' came the call shortly afterwards, and the performers emerged in ones and twos to take their places on the stage. The corridor was a narrow one, and Freddy flattened himself against the wall to allow everyone to pass. The door to the room occupied by Desirée and Jenny Minter opened, and Jenny emerged, followed, somewhat to Freddy's surprise, by Max D'Auberville, the writer and producer of *Consider the Ravens*, who was saying, 'That's quite all right, no hurry at all. I'll bring you the papers tomorrow, and we'll discuss matters further.'

'Do,' replied Jenny. D'Auberville clasped her hand warmly and left through the stage door, while Jenny flashed a smile at Freddy, indicated that she would speak to him later, and disappeared towards the stage.

At length the music began and the curtain went up, and Freddy was alone to look around as he wished. He considered watching the show from the wings, as he had on the night of Septimus's death, but decided against it as several of the cast were already there, awaiting their cues to go on, and he did not wish to be in the way. He regarded the door to Loveday's dressing-room thoughtfully. It was situated between the room occupied by Trenton and Morry Jinks on one side, and Jenny and Desirée on the other. Freddy went into Trenton's room and knocked on the wall, wondering how easily voices carried between the rooms. It seemed solid enough. After that he went into Loveday's room and found Alice the dresser there, folding clothes and tidying up.

'I beg your pardon, I don't mean to intrude,' he said. 'I'm here on Miss Minter's instructions. I'm supposed to be writing a piece on Mr. Gooch. You were the one who found him, weren't you?'

'Yes, sir, and it gave me such a turn!' she replied. 'Forty-two years I've worked in the theatre and I've never seen anything like it. The sight of him lying there staring at me as though he'd seen the Devil—why, it makes me sick to think of it! I nearly died of fright. I thought there'd been evil deeds a-doing.'

'Miss Curtis thinks he was frightened to death by an apparition, doesn't she?'

'I shouldn't wonder,' she said. 'There's all sorts of talk of spirits and phantoms hereabouts. For myself I take care never to be here alone at night.'

'You believe the theatre is haunted?'

'If it wasn't before, it will be now after all these goings-on,' she said ominously. 'I shouldn't be surprised if the spirit of Mr. Gooch himself were to walk abroad.'

'But Mr. Gooch couldn't have been killed by his own ghost,' Freddy pointed out.

'Well, no, I dare say you're right,' she conceded.

'Miss Curtis complained of hearing voices. Did you hear them too?'

'Oh yes, sir!' she replied, to Freddy's surprise, for Loveday had told him she had been the only one. 'Terrible, they were! A-hissing and a-whispering who knows what until a body didn't know where to turn.'

'Good Lord! What did they say?' he asked.

'I couldn't tell you exactly what they said, because I didn't hear them myself, but Miss Curtis heard them right enough. Terrified, she was, and rightly so—who knows but what the evil spirits mightn't have come for her next, to carry her off into the next world.'

'Do you agree with Miss Curtis that Mr. Gooch met an apparition and died of shock, then?'

'Well, not to say agree. Perhaps he did. Although there's some what say he fell over when he was in his cups, and others what say he never touched a drop and slipped over acciden-tally. I think it might have been one or the other.'

'Do you think someone could have hit him and knocked him over?'

'Oh yes, I expect they did, sir.'

Freddy gave it up. It was evident that had he suggested an elephant had strolled in through the stage door and dashed Septimus Gooch to the floor with its trunk, she would have agreed with that too.

He left her fussing over her work and went to explore a little. Jenny and Desirée's dressing-room was at the end of the corridor closest to the stage. Between it and the wings a short flight of three or four steps led up to the right, and from there the corridor continued along the back of the stage. It was dim and difficult to see, but Freddy made out more dressing-rooms, most of their doors ajar. He put his head into one of them. It was much more spacious than the rooms currently occupied by the cast, but was unusable at present, since most of the furniture and fixtures had been removed and the walls stripped down to the bare plaster, while the linoleum had been partly pulled up to reveal dusty boards underneath. A bucket full of broken tiles stood on a shabby old table, and various tools were littered about the place. Freddy withdrew and looked into another room. This one must have previously been occupied by the chorus, for it was much larger than the others, with a looking-glass running along the whole of one wall and several chairs stacked neatly in the corner. It was nearer completion than the first room but still unfinished. A door leading off it at the near end bore a sign which said 'DO NOT ENTER.' Freddy glanced in and saw a small cloak-room containing a lavatory and a wash-basin. The fittings were new, but the wall was of bare plaster and the floor tiles only partly laid, and in the dim light he could see pipes protruding here and there.

'Fell out with the builders, didn't 'e?' came a voice behind Freddy, making him start. It was the stage door-keeper. He joined Freddy and surveyed the dressing-room dispassionately.

'He was an old twister, he was. Always trying to get something for nothing.'

'Septimus, you mean?' asked Freddy. 'Is that why the work isn't finished?'

Alf nodded.

'He got a feller in and they agreed a price and then he went back on it. Said they'd done something to his misliking, but if you ask me he was just trying it on.' He wheezed with laughter. 'Should have seen the two of them, snorting and puffing like two angry bulls. The builder chap was half the size of Septimus but he wasn't giving in—not likely. And in the end he had the upper hand, didn't he? 'Cause he was the one with the men and the plaster, and he told his men to down tools and go home, because he wasn't going to have any more of it until he'd been paid. And there it got left.'

'The builders never came back? How long ago was this?'

Alf sniffed.

'Back in the summer. All modern lights and plumbing, we was to have. This place was built with the insurance money from the last one but it was done quickly and on the cheap and needed doing again. That's what happens when you cut corners. You have to do it twice. Well, much good it did him.'

'So everyone is having to cram into tiny rooms in the other corridor until the builder gets paid,' said Freddy. 'This is where the chorus used to live, I gather. Isn't it where Una Bryant died?'

'Naw, they'd all moved out of this room by then. They're not allowed to come up here now on pain of sacking—too many sharp edges, and Septimus didn't want the plaster dust ruining their costumes. They found her in the other room down there.' He jerked a thumb in the direction of the stage door corridor.

'It's not Una who's been haunting the place, is it?'

'Haunting? Who says anybody's been haunting the place?'

'Mainly Miss Curtis, as far as I can tell, although I hear

other people have reported that their things have gone missing or been moved.'

'They're imagining things,' said Alf. 'Nobody'll haunt this theatre while I'm in charge.'

'You don't believe in ghosts?'

'Perhaps I do. But not the sort you mean.'

'What sort, then?'

Alf glared suspiciously at Freddy.

'None of your business. What d'you want to know all this for, anyway?'

'I'm here for Miss Minter,' replied Freddy. 'She thinks there's something odd about the way Septimus died.'

'Does she, now? She's a good girl, Jen, but she oughter leave well alone. No good can come of it.' Alf's eyes became misty with reminiscence. 'Me and her go back years, all the way to the music hall, in the days when I was still on the boards before my voice went. Jacinta Moreno, she called herself. She had a Spanish act, with the flamenco dancing and the castanets, but as English as you or I, of course. A beautiful girl, she was—still is. She was too good for Septimus, and I told her so. But she would have her own way, and look what good it did her. What did she ever get out of it?'

'All his money,' said Freddy before he could stop himself.

''Ere, what are you suggesting?'

'Nothing at all,' replied Freddy hurriedly. 'I merely meant that now he's gone, perhaps Miss Minter will be slightly more amenable to the demands of the builder and the work will get finished.'

'Maybe,' conceded Alf. 'She's a head for business, Jenny has—as good as any man's. And she won't trample all over them like Septimus did, she'll talk 'em round nicely.'

'Look here, what do you think happened to Septimus? Did you see anything that night?'

'Like what?'

'Well, you were up and down the corridor during the

second act when you weren't in your box or standing in the wings. Did you see anybody go into Loveday's room?'

'I wouldn't tell you if I did—I know how to keep my trap shut. But as it happened, I didn't.'

'You didn't see anything suspicious at all?'

'Not a thing. And believe me, if there'd been anything to see I'd have seen it.'

There was no use in contradicting him, as it was evident he had his story and was determined not to budge from it. The stage door-keeper gave one last look around the bare dressing-room and turned to leave.

'If you arst me, it was an accident,' he said over his shoulder as he went out.

Chapter Seven

A FEW MINUTES before the interval Rupert St. Clair crooned
the last line of his sentimental hit song *I'd Swim An Ocean For
You*, received his due applause and made his exit from the
stage as the rest of the cast launched smoothly into the dance
number which closed the first act. Freddy, standing just
offstage, was treated to a gust of mingled whisky and grease-
paint as Rupert swept past.

'Come and have a chat, won't you?' Rupert said over his
shoulder. Freddy followed him into his dressing-room and
looked around. The place was comfortable enough, if slightly
cramped. It was smaller than the room occupied by Loveday
Curtis, and had space only for an armchair rather than a sofa.
Photographs of Rupert himself—sometimes alone, sometimes
in company with other notable personalities—adorned the
walls, and it seemed Rupert was as fond of flowers as Loveday
was, to judge by the number of delicate and expensive
arrangements which stood on almost every surface.

'*So* tiresome having to exist in this rabbit hutch,' said
Rupert carelessly. 'Do sit. Cigarette?' He lit one for himself, sat
down before the glass and began looking at himself critically
from various angles.

Freddy lowered himself into the armchair, which was softer than it looked and sank alarmingly beneath him. Rupert concluded the examination of his own features and regarded Freddy's reflection sharply.

'I understand Jenny has invited you in to write a puff on Septimus,' he said. 'If you want a quote you may tell the world he was a fine man and will be sorely missed by his many friends in the theatre.' He turned and eyed Freddy directly. 'If you want the truth, however, he was a villain, a wretch, a blight upon humanity. Call it whatever you like—just don't print it.'

'Shouldn't dream of it,' said Freddy cheerfully. 'You weren't fond of him, then?'

Rupert raised his eyes to heaven and gave a shudder.

'My dear boy, you've no idea of the sheer ghastliness one has to put up with at times in this business.'

'I can imagine.'

'Can you? I very much doubt you can. I could tell you stories that would make your hair stand on end, but since one must at least put on a *pretence* of showing respect for the dead, I won't press all the gory details upon you. From a professional point of view, however, I have no hesitation in confiding that even leaving aside his foul character, Septimus hadn't the first idea of how to stage a show.'

'Really? I thought he was rather successful.'

Rupert waved a hand.

'Oh, I don't deny he had a certain animal cunning. He was sharp enough to recognize that he lacked any true under-standing of the business, and learned very early on to ride the coat-tails of the real talent.'

'Such as yourself?'

'Kind of you—naturally, one hesitates to apply the word to oneself. But as it happens I wasn't referring only to my own provocations. I'm not the only person to have been forced to suffer the fellow. He fastened on to people and sucked them dry for his own purposes. He was nothing more or less than a leech.'

'I say,' said Freddy.

'You might well do. At any rate, I'd had quite enough of him.'

'Ah yes, Trenton said you were about to leave the show.'

'I was indeed. Septimus and I disagreed strongly over my interpretation of Walter Wordsworth—my character in *Have At It!* you know. He'd no understanding of Walter's motivation. He thought the scene in which the pirates force me to walk the plank was a mere comic interlude, which of course one can't deny, since it is rather funny, but he simply wouldn't understand the deeper struggle going on under the surface. I see the scene as very much showing Walter's doubts as to whether his love for Annabel is strong enough to survive, and the moment in which I take a flying leap into the abyss represents my decision to relinquish all attempts to control something which is essentially uncontrollable.'

Freddy blinked, remembering the scene, at which he had laughed heartily.

'I see,' he said.

Rupert went on:

'"I know it's just a light musical, Septimus," I said, "but really one must be professional and *get things right*. We can't get away with offering second-rate entertainment to the paying customers, no matter how ignorant and unwashed they may be. Jim Higgins's money is every bit as good as Lord Folderol's, and he knows what he likes—besides, there are many more Higginses than Folderols in the world, so one must cater to them if one's to make a success of things." Anyway, it was perfectly obvious we were never going to agree, so I told him I should have to leave.'

'Ah, then I must have been mistaken. I understood he hadn't renewed your contract.'

'That couldn't be less true,' snapped Rupert. 'It was quite

my decision. When one's been in the business a while one learns to recognize when it's time to move on.'

'What shall you do next?'

Rupert waved his cigarette.

'I've a number of irons in the fire. It's just a question of deciding which part to take. Perhaps I might even take a short holiday—but I shan't stay away too long. One doesn't wish to disappoint one's public.'

'You were angry with Septimus on the night he died and were looking for him just before the second act. Mind telling me what you wanted to speak to him about?'

'Was I angry? I don't remember. I expect it wasn't anything very serious, and I certainly wasn't cross for long. I never am. I'm known throughout the business for my equable temperament. You'll barely get a brusque word out of me.'

'Then you didn't speak to him in the end?'

'No. I stayed in my room until I heard the call. I don't go on immediately and I know I have exactly fifteen minutes until I have to be on stage after the first call, so they don't always bother knocking on my door—but this time when I came out Artie started hissing at me that I was late so I rushed on to do my bit and wouldn't have had time to speak to Septimus if I'd wanted to. I come on with *The Old Vo-Do-De-Oh*, you'll remember. A simple tune, you'd think, but much more complicated to sing than you might imagine. This part, you know—' He hummed a few bars of the tune. 'An odd little arpeggio, and not as easy as it sounds. Then when we all came off old Alice started screaming that Septimus was dead. I shouldn't have wished it on him, but I confess I've been completely unable to squeeze out so much as a tear.'

He eyed Freddy speculatively.

'Do come to my flat for a drink some time. I've rather a fondness for your fine publication. They sent a young reporter round a year or two ago when I was doing *A Smile For Summer* at the Alhambra—I dare say you remember the show. What

was his name, now? Reggie or Ronnie something. Jolliffe—
that was his name, yes. Delightful young man. I gave him a
personal tour of my collection of Imperial Vienna and Sèvres
porcelain and he was most fascinated.'

Freddy thought he remembered the occasion. Jolliffe had
returned from his assignment slightly pale in the face, saying
quite firmly that he would very much rather not visit Rupert
St. Clair alone in his flat again. Then he had refused to say
anything else but sat down to write the piece with a set jaw.

The rest of the cast had come off for the interval now, and
Jenny came in wanting to speak to Rupert, so Freddy took his
leave before Rupert could press the invitation. Outside he saw
Artie Jennings the stage-manager standing in the doorway of
Trenton and Morry Jinks's room, talking to them about some
aspect of the performance. Freddy considered him for a
second, but was sure Artie had not gone anywhere near the
stage door corridor in the vital period on the night in question, and so would certainly not have had time to commit a
murder. He turned to see Desirée just coming out of her
dressing-room.

'Jenny says you want to speak to us all for an obituary
you're writing,' she said.

'That's right. Do you have a moment now?'

Desirée looked doubtful.

'I suppose so, although I don't know what she wants me to
say.' She led him back into the dressing-room. 'I didn't know
Septimus at all well, but if you like you can count me among
the "sadly missed by all those who knew him." Isn't that the
kind of thing you say in these articles?'

'Something like that. But is it true? Will you miss him
sadly?'

'What do you mean?' she said, going a little pink under
her make-up.

'I rather thought he'd been making a nuisance of himself.'

She went pinker.

'Is that what Trenton said?'

'He mentioned something of the sort. I think he's a trifle concerned about you.'

'Trenton's a dear boy,' she said carelessly. 'He rather fancies himself as my protector. But there's no need at all. I'm quite capable of looking after myself.'

'Then it's true? About Septimus, I mean?'

'Certainly not!'

The reply and the haughty look that accompanied it said emphatically that she had no intention of admitting to anything of the sort. Her attempt at worldly sophistication did not fool Freddy for a second, but he did not press the point.

'Odd, the way Septimus died suddenly just like that,' he observed instead.

'Was it? I suppose it was.'

'I gather he had a good few enemies. If this were a sixpenny novel then there'd be a detective grubbing around on the floor of Loveday's dressing-room with a magnifying glass by now, and another asking everyone whether they had an alibi.'

She laughed.

'Well, my alibi is straightforward enough. I didn't go into Loveday's room at all on the night he died.'

Freddy wagged a finger affably.

'Aha, but can you prove it? Where were you between the time when Septimus was last seen, and the moment his body was found?'

'Onstage, of course.'

'But before that? During the interval, I mean.'

'Why, I—' She paused. 'I was running a little late. It was my own fault—I'd been trying out a new type of paint stick that night, but when I came offstage I realized it was quite unsuitable—it had run under the lights and gone very streaky. But I didn't realize how bad it was until almost the end of the interval, and I had to clean it off in a hurry while everybody else was waiting in the wings to go back on. Luckily I don't go on immediately, so I had a few minutes to do it. I'd just finished when my ceiling light blew out, so I went to find Alf and ask him to fix it. Then I came back and went onstage.'

'Who can confirm that?'

'Well, Alf saw me when I spoke to him about the light. I found him on the other corridor. You can ask him if you like. But other than that, nobody, as far as I know.'

'What about during the second act itself? You weren't on all the time, were you? You come off once or twice.'

'Yes, but I run to the dressing-room, change in a tearing hurry, and rush back on practically still fastening my buttons up. I certainly don't have time to stop and chat with anybody, let alone kill someone.' She gave him a curious look. 'But this is all a joke, of course, isn't it? I mean, Septimus wasn't really murdered, was he?'

'Not as far as I know,' replied Freddy.

And indeed it was true. He had done as Jenny requested and asked questions, but he felt he was casting around in the dark. What exactly was there to ask? How could he come to any conclusion if he had no idea what had caused Septimus to fall and bang his head? Freddy rubbed his ear discontentedly. As investigations went, it was proving highly unsatisfactory so far.

Chapter Eight

THE SHOW ENDED and the cast thronged off the stage. Freddy hung around, wanting to speak to Jenny alone. At length she emerged from her dressing-room.

'Do come in,' she said. 'Desirée's gone.' She looked at him inquiringly as she shut the door behind them. 'Well?'

He shook his head.

'Nothing so far. I've spoken to almost everyone, and the most I can glean is that he wasn't especially popular—although I expect you knew that—and that nobody has given much thought to his death at all.'

'What about Una?'

'I haven't had a chance to ask about her yet.'

'You'd better speak to the chorus about her, as they knew her better than anybody. Ask for Peggy—she's a sensible girl and will answer your questions without squealing or giggling, unlike some of the others.'

Freddy promised to do as she said and took his leave. He came out of the dressing-room and glanced up and down the deserted corridor. The two biggest rooms in this area were allocated to the chorus, and he knocked hesitantly on the door of one of them.

'No use knocking, they've all gone home,' came Alf's voice behind him. 'And you keep your hands orf 'em,' he added sternly.

'Your implication wounds me deeply,' said Freddy, for the look of the thing.

Everyone seemed to have gone, so he decided to follow suit. He would have to return to the theatre another time to speak to the girls of the chorus and find out more about Una Bryant. He had not gone far along the alley, however, when he was accosted by two figures who emerged smoothly from the shadows and attached themselves to him, one on each arm. It was the twins.

'Hallo,' he said. 'You weren't waiting for me, were you?'

'We didn't want to be wandering around alone in the dark,' said one. He thought it was Maudie.

'Perfectly understandable,' replied Freddy. 'I don't much like it myself. Where can I take you?'

'Oh, not far,' said the one he thought was Minnie.

They walked in silence for a few minutes, then Maudie yawned.

'Lord, I'm tired,' she said.

'Too many late nights, I expect.'

She waved a hand dismissively.

'We get up late. There's no matinée on Tuesdays, so we've plenty of time to catch up.' She threw Freddy a sideways glance. 'As a matter of fact, we thought you might like to take us for lunch tomorrow.'

Freddy had been expecting something of the sort.

'Did you, now?'

'You will, won't you?' said Minnie, gazing up at him beseechingly on his other side.

'Hmm. Let me think. Where should you like to go?'

'What about the Ritz?' she said hopefully.

'The Ritz, eh? That's jolly expensive. What do I get out of it?'

They giggled.

'Why, the pleasure of our company, of course.'

'I'm not exactly welcome at the Ritz at present,' said Freddy, musing. 'There was an incident a couple of months ago that wasn't my fault. Or at least not entirely. But I'll take you to lunch and welcome.'

They finally settled on a more modest yet still pleasant establishment.

'See you tomorrow then,' said Maudie as they parted. 'Don't be late.'

'As neat a job as ever I saw,' remarked Freddy, who wished it to be known that he was no fool.

They giggled again and melted into the night. Freddy shook his head and went home.

He turned up for his engagement in good time the next day, for he was almost certain the invitation to lunch had been more than just a friendly overture. His suspicions were confirmed when he arrived at the appointed place to find not two, but four girls already waiting for him: the twins, Peggy, and a dainty girl with fluffy blonde hair peeking out from a pert blue hat. They were seated at a corner table, talking together in low voices, but looked up when he arrived.

'Quite a party, what?' he said.

'We thought you wouldn't mind,' said Minnie, or possibly Maudie. 'Do you know Peggy? And this is Dinah.'

'Charmed,' said the blonde girl delicately, as Peggy nodded at him.

They all shuffled around and he found himself seated between the twins. He had no idea which was which, but decided for the sake of convenience to assume they were sitting in alphabetical order by name facing the door, and that therefore Maudie was on his right. There was some delay as they decided upon their food, then once the waiter had departed, Minnie looked around and said:

'Well, isn't this lovely?'

'Rather,' agreed Maudie.

'Quite delightful,' said Freddy affably. 'And now that the formalities are out of the way, which of you would like to tell me why we're really here?'

They all looked at Peggy, who seemed to be the leader.

'Maudie said you'd been asking about Mr. Gooch and Una, and about how they died,' Peggy said. 'Did Jenny ask you to find out?'

'She did, as a matter of fact.'

'Does she think somebody did it deliberately? I know Loveday thinks Mr. Gooch was frightened to death by a ghost, but that's not really true, is it?'

'Why do you ask?'

'Because it's ridiculous!'

'It does seem so,' agreed Freddy. He waited.

'It's just—' began Peggy.

The girls all glanced at one another.

'Just what?' inquired Freddy.

'I've seen the ghost!' Dinah burst out. 'And you've seen it too,' she said accusingly to Peggy.

'It wasn't a ghost,' said Peggy unconvincingly.

'Well, then, what was it?' demanded Dinah.

'I don't know.'

They all began to speak at once, and Freddy held up a hand.

'One at a time, please. Tell me what you saw, and when.'

'It was on the day Una died,' began Dinah, ignoring a warning look from Peggy. 'We've always known the theatre's been haunted ever since it burned down a hundred years ago.'

'Twenty-five years ago, I believe,' said Freddy.

'Well, that's still practically a century,' said Dinah, who could not have been more than nineteen. 'They say the place went up in flames, and lots of people were dreadfully burned, and a famous actor died.'

'I heard he disappeared into the flames trying to rescue the leading lady. It was ever so romantic,' put in Maudie.

'Did the leading lady die too?' asked Freddy.

Maudie shrugged.

'I don't know. I think perhaps she got out. She must have, or there'd have been two ghosts, wouldn't there?'

Minnie said, with a pleasurable shiver:

'They say whoever sees the ghost will die within days.'

'Who's *they*?'

'I don't know. I just heard it somewhere. Of course, it's all tales, really. Show-people are terribly superstitious but it's mostly just fun.'

'No it's not,' said Dinah. 'There are ghosts, I tell you! I've seen lots of them.'

'What was it you saw at the Jollity, exactly?' asked Freddy.

'It was Una who saw it first,' replied Dinah. 'On the night she died we were getting ready before the show, and she came into the dressing-room and said she'd just seen what she was sure was the Jollity ghost disappearing along the corridor that runs behind the stage.'

'What was she doing on that corridor? I thought it was out of bounds.'

'Now you've gone and done it,' said Peggy to Dinah. She turned to Freddy. 'We used to use the lav. there even though old Gooch threatened to fire us if we did. There were too many people sharing the tiny one on the stage door corridor, and the one in our old room was nice and new, even though they never finished the work. But please don't tell Jenny or anyone, or we'll be in trouble.'

'I won't,' Freddy assured her.

Dinah resumed her tale.

'Una said she was just coming out of the cloak-room when there was a movement in the corner of her eye, and she turned and saw a mysterious figure disappearing into the distance at the far end of the corridor.'

'A stage-hand or someone?' suggested Freddy.

'It was nobody she recognized. It was tall and thin, and a sort of powdery grey. Of course, I knew immediately it must be the ghost. Don't you see? The powder is the ash from the fire all those years ago. It must be! It can't be anything else. The man who died is haunting the theatre to this day!'

'You do talk nonsense,' said Peggy.

Dinah ignored her and went on.

'I told Una not to go back into the corridor because of the curse, but she laughed and said she didn't believe in that sort of thing and she was sure she was a match for any ghost.'

'And did she go back?'

'I—' began Dinah, glancing at Peggy.

'No,' said Peggy firmly. 'We all went on stage then, and she came back with us for the interval.'

'But she didn't come on stage again with you for the second act?' said Freddy.

'We thought she did,' answered Minnie. 'We were in a bit of a rush what with one thing and another, and Artie was calling us, and we hurried on, and I honestly thought she was there too for most of the second act, because we don't do anything in strict sequence until later on so we didn't notice she was missing. But once we did Peggy got worried, so we missed our final bows and went to look for her. Well, we found her all right.'

They all looked distressed.

'She was lying on the floor of your dressing-room, I understand.'

'Yes,' said Peggy shortly.

'And nobody knows what killed her. But why do you think a ghost had anything to do with it?'

'We didn't really—not seriously, I mean—until the night Mr. Gooch died,' replied Dinah. 'That night before the show Peggy and I went to use the new lavatory—I didn't like to go alone, you see, what with the place being haunted. And when we came out we saw exactly what Una saw on the night of her death—a tall, thin figure, all dusty grey, limping away from us along the corridor, moaning softly.'

'Is that what you saw?' said Freddy turning to Peggy, whom he judged to be the less credulous of the two.

'Something of the kind,' she admitted reluctantly.

'So you see, the stories are true!' exclaimed Dinah. 'Una saw the ghost and *then she died*. And the next time the ghost came, Mr. Gooch died too!'

'Did Mr. Gooch see the ghost?' asked Freddy.

'I've no idea, but Peggy and I saw it, so it was there all right.'

'But you're not dead,' Freddy pointed out.

'Not yet,' said Minnie darkly.

Dinah gave a squeak. She seemed genuinely frightened.

'I'm scared, Peggy,' she said. 'What if it was our fault?'

They all glanced at one another.

'Who else has seen the ghost?' asked Freddy. 'Anyone else?'

'A few of the other girls seem to think they have,' replied Peggy, 'but I'm pretty sure they haven't. They can't describe it, or they say it's a woman all dressed in white and wearing chains—the usual stuff. They've active imaginations and you know how excitable girls can be. None of them saw the man we saw.'

'We haven't seen it,' said Minnie and Maudie, apparently with regret.

Freddy said to Dinah:

'Should you have thought he was a ghost if Una hadn't said so?'

She opened her eyes wide.

'Why, yes. It's not just the figure, you see. Other things have happened too. Things have been moved around.'

'Ah, yes, one of the twins lost a scarf, didn't you?'

'Yes,' said Maudie. 'I left it on the little sofa in our dressing-room when I left the theatre after the show, and found it on a shelf the next day, all nicely folded up. That sort of thing has happened a few times.'

'A tidy ghost, then. Perhaps you ought to keep it. And you're sure you haven't heard any of these voices I keep hearing about?'

'Quite sure,' they all answered firmly at once.

They seemed certain enough of that, at least.

'Very well, then,' said Freddy. 'Let's say for the fun of it that the theatre really is haunted and by some strange means a ghost has been striking down actors and producers willy-nilly. But what is it you want me to do about it? I mean to say, I should have thought an exorcist would be more useful in the case than a reporter.'

'We just thought you might be able to find out what it was that killed Una,' said Peggy at last. 'We'd like to—that is, I'd feel better if we could be sure there's nothing we could have done to save her.'

Something in her manner drew his attention.

'There's something you're not telling me,' he said. 'What is it?'

'There's nothing, I promise,' she replied, shaking her head. 'It's just they couldn't even say at the inquest what killed her, and now Mr. Gooch is dead, and we've been wondering whether the same thing mightn't have killed them both. Morry Jinks said Jenny told him you were to write an obituary for Mr. Gooch, but he reckoned that was rot, and that she really asked you to find out how he died.'

'That's true,' admitted Freddy.

'Well, we'd like you to find out how Una died as well. She was a friend of ours and we liked her, and it's not fair that old Gooch gets all the attention when nobody liked him anyway, while Una gets forgotten because she wasn't as important or as rich as he was. I don't really believe in ghosts, but if there *was* something…'

Her voice tailed off.

Freddy looked around the table. Four pairs of eyes were fixed on him in appeal. Having found out very little so far, he had been more or less intending to retire gracefully from the investigation, but it was difficult to resist the pleas of these four girls who had lost their friend.

'I'll do what I can,' he said.

They beamed.

'I told you he'd be all right, didn't I?' said Maudie.

'Well, I can't promise anything, but I'll do my best,' said Freddy. 'So, then, where are we? Two people have died in mysterious circumstances, you've seen a ghost but haven't heard any voices, and Loveday has heard voices but hasn't seen a ghost.'

There was a certain snorting and wrinkling of the nose at the mention of Loveday.

'You don't seem to like Miss Curtis,' Freddy observed.

Peggy grimaced.

'Not much.'

'Why not?'

'She danced in the chorus like us until last year,' explained Maudie. 'She and Peggy were best friends for ever such a long time, weren't you?'

'We practically grew up together,' agreed Peggy.

'I gather you fell out,' Freddy hazarded.

'She stole Peggy's part!' said Minnie hotly, as Peggy glowered.

'I say, not really?'

'Yes,' said Maudie. 'It was a dirty trick.'

Freddy looked at Peggy inquiringly.

'Loveday and I were sharing digs last year,' she said, 'and the two of us were in the final running for the lead in *Just A*

Mo. We'd both done three or four auditions, but they really liked me and told me privately the part was as good as in the bag. They invited me back to do one last try-out with the leading man, and I was so sure this was it, and that I was going to get out of the chorus at last.'

'What happened?'

'I made the mistake of telling Loveday what they'd said. I knew it was hard luck on her but I thought she wouldn't mind, us being friends and all. But it seems she couldn't stand the idea of losing out to me and wanted that part by hook or by crook. Anyway, I'd been out all day and the audition was supposed to be the next morning, but when I came home Loveday told me there'd been a message to say the time had been changed from ten o'clock to four in the afternoon.'

'That was a lie, I assume.'

'What do you think? The more fool I for believing her,' said Peggy bitterly. 'Of course she just happened to be at the theatre at the right time while they were waiting for me, stepped in and did the try-out in my place, and got the part. And all I got for my pains was a reputation for not turning up.'

'Oh, poor show,' said Freddy sympathetically.

'She lords it over us now,' said Minnie. 'You'd think she'd never shared a dressing-room in her life.'

'And it's not as though she's as talented as you,' added Dinah loyally. 'Her voice hardly carries to the back of the auditorium. You're a much better singer, Peggy.'

'Oh well,' said Peggy. 'Anyway, never mind that—we're not here to talk about Loveday.'

'How do you suggest I go about tracking down this ghost of yours, then?' Freddy asked.

'Peggy and I can show you where we saw it,' answered Dinah. 'We could go after lunch if you like.'

'I can't,' said Peggy. 'I'm supposed to be meeting someone at half past two. You show him.'

This was agreed upon. Their food arrived and conversation turned to other people and other matters of concern. It turned out there had been much talk about Trenton and Desirée, and small amounts had even been wagered over whether it would ever come to anything. Trenton's feelings were perfectly obvious, although it was harder to say whether they were reciprocated. It was generally agreed that Desirée was worried about something, but they did not know what.

'Odd how theatre people always seem to be drawn together,' observed Freddy. 'I mean to say, one doesn't often see an actress married to a blacksmith or a fishmonger.'

'I've found it's better to stick with one's own type,' replied Dinah, with an air of worldly wisdom. 'I was friendly with someone in the building trade for a little while once, but I had to end it as we didn't see eye to eye.'

'He was working at the Jollity and fell head over heels in love with her,' confided Minnie, as Dinah tossed her head. 'But that sort don't understand show-business. They're drawn in by the glamour at first, but after a while they start to get jealous. Maybe a girl has a part where she has to kiss another man every night. They don't like that. Then they start to complain because she has to work evenings and gets home late, and at last they say, "It's either the theatre or me," and that's when it all comes to an end.'

'It was a pity, because I did rather like him,' said Dinah. 'He knew a lot of interesting things, but we didn't have much in common, so I had to finish it. As a matter of fact I was pleased when Mr. Gooch sent the builders away, because he didn't take it especially well and things were a little awkward between us.'

'But what if Jenny brings them back?' said Maudie. 'She might now old Gooch is dead. Then you'll have to see him again.'

Peggy laughed.

'I reckon Jenny's got other things on her mind. Did you see Max D'Auberville smarming around her last night?'

'I saw him,' said Freddy. 'I didn't know they knew one another.'

'I heard he and Mr. Gooch were partners at one time. I expect he wanted to talk about business with her,' said Dinah.

'It looked like more than business to me,' said Peggy. 'He was really laying it on thick. If you ask me he's been looking for an opportunity to worm his way into her good books behind old Gooch's back for a while now. Joyce told me she saw him coming out of Jenny's dressing-room the other week. I reckon he's after her money.'

'He's very good-looking,' said Maudie. 'I don't wonder she likes it.'

'Too clever for my liking,' said Minnie. 'I shouldn't be able to keep up with the conversation. His plays are very difficult to understand, they say. Alf told me they were metaphorical, but I don't really know what that means.'

'I saw *Far Hope* a few years ago,' said Peggy. 'I thought it was rather good.'

'Didn't you find it a trifle turgid?' asked Freddy in surprise.

'Peggy's an *intellectual*, aren't you, Peggy?' said Maudie slyly.

'There's nothing wrong with educating yourself,' replied Peggy with dignity.

Once lunch had ended and the bill had been settled to Freddy's disadvantage, Minnie said:

'It's our birthday on Saturday and we're going to the Copernicus Club after the show to celebrate. Would you like to come?'

'Oh, do,' said Maudie. 'It's going to be so much fun!'

They all chorused the invitation, and Freddy, who was easily tempted by the prospect of heedless amusement, promised to come. Then they all stood up and prepared to leave.

'Let's go to the Jollity and see what we can find,' said Freddy to Dinah.

The doorway of the restaurant was a narrow one, and there was a general crowding together and a certain amount of confusion as they stumbled out into the street, where they bumped into Gertie of all people, who was just passing. She regarded the group in surprise as Freddy disentangled himself from the twins, who were clinging to his arms and laughing up at him.

'Ah, hallo, Gertie,' he said. 'You remember *Have At It!* don't you? We saw it the other week. And those marvellous back-somersaults across the deck of the ship. Well, these are the girls who do them.'

'How lovely,' said Gertie politely. 'It must take an awful lot of practice.'

'It does,' replied Peggy with equal politeness, as the other girls regarded Gertie with undisguised interest, taking in everything from her darling little French hat to her silk stockings at nineteen and six a pair.

There was a short silence as it began to dawn on Freddy that it might not be entirely unreasonable for a young lady of noble birth to be somewhat irked upon discovering her swain spilling unsteadily out of a Soho restaurant in company with four giggling chorus-girls in cheap fur coats. Gertie made no remark to that effect, however, but merely said, 'Don't forget dinner on Thursday,' then sailed off.

'That's Lady Gertrude McAloon,' said Maudie as they watched her go. 'I've seen her in the papers. She's awfully chic, isn't she? Do you know her?'

'You might say that,' answered Freddy. He was half-wondering whether to chase after her and explain, but decided it would look awkward. Gertie was not the jealous type, and he was fairly confident that she was also not the sort to jump to unwarranted conclusions upon little evidence.

'Shall we go?' he said, turning back to the girls. As he did so he was just in time to catch a warning look and a hissed 'Remember!' from Peggy to Dinah when she thought he was not looking. From this and one or two incidents during lunch he strongly suspected that there was something they had not told him. He wondered what it was.

Chapter Nine

ALF WAS NOT in his box when they came in through the stage door, and the place seemed deserted, but the sound of hammering indicated that carpenters were at work somewhere.

'Will you show me exactly what you saw and where?' asked Freddy. 'It was in the other corridor, wasn't it?'

Dinah had become increasingly nervous as they approached the Jollity, and seemed to be in two minds about the whole thing.

'Along there,' she replied, pointing. She hung back a little as Freddy passed the dressing-rooms, turned right and went up the short flight of stairs which led to the empty corridor. It looked much as it had when he had come along here the other day, although a small amount of daylight was filtering into the dimness from somewhere and he could see slightly more clearly today.

'It was just there,' said Dinah at his shoulder, indicating a spot a short distance away.

'Where were you standing? Just here, I suppose. This is the dressing-room you all shared before they chucked you out to do the building works, yes? And that's the lavatory just off it.

You and Peggy came out—quietly, I imagine, since you weren't meant to be here.'

'Yes. Artie was talking to Desirée at the bottom of the steps so we waited a moment until he'd gone, and that's when we saw it.'

'But how could you see it clearly? Wasn't it dark?'

'Yes, but there's enough light from the other corridor to see a little.'

'And you're sure it was the figure of a man, not a woman?'

'I think so. It was tall and thin, with a limp.'

'How very odd. Where was it going, do you think?'

'I don't know. We only saw it for a couple of seconds, as we were too busy watching Artie and waiting for him to go away. We didn't even know it was there until it made a sort of groaning noise and we turned and saw it. It gave me such a fright I nearly shrieked the place down, but then Artie would have seen us and given us what for. At any rate, as soon as he'd gone we practically fell down those stairs and ran back to the dressing-room. We had to go on stage a minute after that, then after the show they found Mr. Gooch dead and I was certain it was something to do with the ghost.'

'Ah, yes, I remember your mentioning it that night. Now, what about Una? They've split you into two rooms on the stage door corridor, haven't they? Which one was she in? Where was she found?'

'It was the one at the end,' replied Dinah. 'All five of us were in it together.'

'That's the nearest one to the forbidden corridor. I say, that's rather a good title for a ghost story, don't you think?'

She gave a small smile, although it was clear her heart was not in it. She was twisting a ring nervously on her finger. Freddy decided to take advantage of her evident agitation to try and surprise some information out of her.

'Look here,' he said. 'If you want me to find out what happened to your friend you really ought to tell me the truth.'

'What do you mean? I've told you the truth.'

'I dare say you have, as far as it goes. But perhaps there's something you're holding back. That wouldn't exactly be telling a lie, would it? But you can't expect me to solve the mystery of Una's death if I don't have all the facts at my disposal.'

She hesitated, as though debating whether to speak, and he went on:

'I'm not the tattling sort. If there's something you did that might get you into trouble I can keep it under my hat.'

'Well—' she began, and glanced up at Freddy, who was looking at her encouragingly. She pulled herself together and shook her head. 'There's nothing, truly there isn't. But—' she gazed into the empty dressing-room, chewing her lip as though in thought. 'There is something else I've been wondering about.'

'What is it?'

'It was just something someone mentioned—it was the young man I was friendly with, as a matter of fact—but it didn't occur to me until the other day when I read something that made me remember what he said, although I don't really know how it would work. And I still don't know where the ghost comes in. Perhaps it was a coincidence. Or perhaps I'm wrong altogether. After all, I'm not an expert in these matters.'

'Which matters?' said Freddy, at a loss.

'Oh, never mind. It's nothing.'

Freddy was about to question her further when she turned her head and gave a sharp gasp. 'What's that?'

Freddy listened. A sound was drifting faintly along the passage towards them. It was a man's voice—a beautiful, melodic tenor—singing a song that Freddy recognized as having been popular in the early years of the century. In the silence of the theatre and in the heightened atmosphere there was something quite eerie about it. Even Freddy, not normally a susceptible sort, was affected for a second or two.

'What is it?' said Dinah fearfully, as Freddy went in search of the source of the sound.

'Just a gramophone in the props room,' he replied. 'Look.'

He was standing by an open door towards the far end of the corridor, and after a moment's hesitation she came to peep in. It was a room piled high with old properties from previous shows: shelves full of shoes; clothing rails loaded with costumes; chairs, divans, a statue of Cupid, its gold paint peeling off here and there, clocks, lamps, a Roman centurion's helmet, a stuffed parrot in a cage, assorted tools tangled in among a coil of copper wire, two wicked-looking scimitars, an ornately-decorated Japanese screen. Standing on an old cabinet to the right of the door was the gramophone, on which a record was revolving. As they listened, it wound itself down and stopped.

'It's the ghost!' whispered Dinah. 'How did the music start itself?'

'It didn't,' replied Freddy. 'It was playing when we arrived, only we didn't notice it because we were talking.'

He stared thoughtfully down at the record on the gramophone, then turned and eyed a green-upholstered chair in the style of Queen Anne which looked as though it had been well sat in. Next to it was a fanciful table with a carved pedestal in the shape of a tree trunk and spreading branches, on which stood a little spirit stove, a battered old kettle and a tea-cup.

'Is this where the ghost disappeared that night?' he asked her.

'I don't know,' she replied. 'We didn't stay long enough to find out.'

Through a tiny window high up in the wall a thin beam of sunshine suddenly appeared, in which specks of dust floated gently. As they gazed around in silence, there came a muffled clanking sound. Dinah jumped and gave a squeak.

'It's just the pipes,' Freddy reassured her.

'I don't like it,' she said. 'Need I stay?'

'Not if you don't want to.'

She needed no further prompting, and left. Freddy heard her footsteps retreating along the corridor. He moved a little further into the room, and as he did so something caught on his jacket and pulled a thread. Turning, he saw the steamer trunk which had been in Loveday's room on the night Septimus Gooch died. It was a fine old thing—almost an antique, made of leather which had once been fine but which was now starting to split in places, and finished with metal banding around each edge and at the corners to protect it from the rigours of long-distance travel. He was just bending down to examine it more closely when he heard voices laughing somewhere. He left the props room and went to the far end of the corridor, where he found an open workshop area at the back of the theatre just next to the large doors to the loading entrance. Here, two men were engaged in repairing a piece of scenery.

'You didn't come down this corridor just now, did you?' Freddy asked them.

'Not us, guv,' replied one cheerfully. They seemed incurious as to the reason for his presence, and were evidently busy, so he withdrew and returned to the stage door entrance, where he found Alf.

''Ere, what were you doing frightening young Dinah out of her wits like that?' demanded the door-keeper. 'She came running out just now like a pack of wolves was chasing her.'

'I didn't frighten her,' replied Freddy. 'The gramophone was playing and she thought it was a ghost. But it was you, wasn't it?'

Alf squinted at him suspiciously.

'Maybe. How did you know?'

'The half-empty cup next to the warm stove. Ghosts don't drink tea that I know of.'

Alf gave his wheezing laugh.

'Ha! You're a sharp one. Well, then, there's nothing wrong

with listening to a bit of music. I like to go in there and have some peace and quiet now and again.'

Freddy forbore to remark on the fact that the theatre was currently silent and deserted.

'Dinah says she and Peggy saw a ghostly figure walking along the back corridor on the night Septimus died,' he said instead.

'You don't want to listen to what they say. They're flighty, the lot of them,' Alf replied scornfully. 'Girls! They haven't got half a brain to share between them.'

'Then you think they were imagining it?'

'Just you keep your nose out,' said Alf. 'It's none of your business and there's no harm done.'

'What do you mean?'

'Never you mind. Now listen, I got work to do and you're where you oughtn't to be so get off with you. Scoot!'

He refused to answer any more questions, so Freddy had no choice but to leave.

He returned to the offices of the *Clarion*, thinking. It was all very odd. From the strange events that had occurred at the Jollity he might almost have said there were two or three ghosts, rather than just one. Only Loveday had heard the voices, while nobody except the chorus-girls had reported seeing a ghostly figure. Where the missing belongings came in he could not tell, although it seemed clear to him that the stage door-keeper knew more than he was telling. Alf had worked at the Jollity for many years. Had he known the actor who died in the fire and whose spirit was now thought to haunt the building? Might the deaths of Una Bryant and Septimus Gooch really have been caused by supernatural activity?

Freddy shook himself.

'You ass, you're getting soft in the head,' he told himself. Of course there were no ghosts. There would be some perfectly logical explanation for the unusual occurrences. His task was to find out what had killed Una and Septimus, and the haunting was merely a distraction. It was not until he had returned to the office that he realized he had forgotten to press Dinah on what it was she was hiding, but he was confident he would be able to get it out of her the next time they met.

Chapter Ten

FREDDY WAS busy at the *Clarion* for the rest of the week and almost forgot about the happenings at the Jollity Theatre. It was not until Gertie wanted to know whether he intended to abide by an earlier half-promise and take her out on Saturday that he remembered he was supposed to be going to the twins' birthday party. He doubted Gertie would be too pleased to hear the exact nature of the engagement, so he put on his best regretful expression and told her he had a long piece to write by Monday first thing, and so would be confined to the office for the whole weekend. To his relief she accepted the lie with little more than an impatient remark, although the story was not exactly a convincing one.

At a late hour on Saturday he duly presented himself at the Copernicus Club, where he found the party in full swing and already becoming rather riotous. The lesser cast members and most of the orchestra were there. Minnie and Maudie, dressed in identical green dresses, were dancing exuberantly, one with the trumpeter and the other with the saxophonist. Freddy, who had made a number of stops at various favoured drinking establishments on his way to the club and was already comfortably lubricated, furnished himself with another drink and found himself in conversation with Trenton, who was in a similar condition. Desirée was not there, and Trenton was inclined to be maudlin and sentimental.

'She's far too good for me, Freddy,' he bellowed into Freddy's ear, since the music was very loud. 'And yet I can't forget her or let her go. Tell me, do you think I've any chance?'

'You'd be better off asking her that rather than me, old bean.'

'It's all very well saying that, but I've already tried that and she ran away.'

'Did she?'

Trenton stared dolefully at his glass.

'Oh, it started well enough. We were walking in the park —friendly-like, you know—and I'd just got up the nerve to say something, but I'd barely got halfway through the sentence when she gave a sort of squeak and ran off.'

'That doesn't sound hopeful.'

'It was discouraging, to put it mildly. When I saw her later she begged pardon and told me she'd suddenly remembered she'd forgotten to lock her front door, but there was no reason she couldn't have told me that before she took off like a rabbit. I dare say it was just an excuse. I mean to say, what could she possibly see in a poor sort of chap like me? She's probably got someone else already, in fact. I expect he's rich and good-looking and knows how to talk to girls without repelling them so much that they make a bolt for it.'

He gazed sadly into his drink.

'Come now, there's no need for that sort of talk. Why not give it another try?' suggested Freddy, clapping him on the shoulder encouragingly. 'I expect it was just a misunderstanding. You're a decent fellow. You've got just as much chance as anyone else of catching her attention, but you won't do it unless you say something. After all, what's the worst that can happen?'

'I don't know. She might burst out laughing. Or make that

noise people make when they're about to be sick. Or she might scream and faint. Or she might pack her things and flee the country in the night. There are any number of ways she could torture and humiliate me.'

'None of them particularly likely, however. She's a nice girl and I'm sure she'd be kind even if the answer were no.'

'That would be the worst thing of all, somehow, to be the object of pity.'

'Odd sort of thing to do, though, running off,' said Freddy. 'Perhaps she really had forgotten to lock the door.'

'To be honest I think she's a little nervy,' replied Trenton. 'She always seems to be looking over her shoulder as though she expects someone to pounce on her. I don't know why. I rather wonder whether old Gooch didn't frighten her with his pestering, although she's perfectly safe from him now.'

He stared ruminatively into his drink then seemed to pull himself together.

'You're right, of course. I won't get anywhere if I don't speak to her. I'll do it next time I see her.' He clapped a hand on Freddy's shoulder and hiccupped loudly. 'You're a good pal, Freddy. It's a pity you and Iris didn't come to anything. I'd far rather have had you than that old stiff Ralph as a brother-in-law.' He lowered his voice confidentially. 'Between you and me, I don't think they're especially well matched.'

'Oh?' said Freddy.

'No. Iris likes to have fun, and there's not much fun going on when Ralph's in the room. Well, she's made her bed and now she must lie in it, but I dare say she'll be happy enough all told, even if he is a bore. She'll be Lady Uttridge or some such one day, and be a society queen bee. She always did like to be looked at.'

'Why are you two skulking in the corner?' said Peggy, coming up to them just then. 'Come and do your dancing duty.'

Freddy was only too happy to oblige. He danced with Peggy, then another member of the chorus, then another.

'I've danced with all of you now, except Dinah,' he said during a slightly unsteady fox-trot with one of the twins (he was not sure which). 'Where is she?'

'Somewhere, I expect,' replied the twin.

'Many happy returns, by the way.'

'Thank you. We're having such fun.'

'Isn't it a little trying, always having to share the attention with someone else on your birthday?'

'Oh, Maudie and I don't mind,' she replied, thereby telling him her name and saving him the necessity of having to admit he still could not tell the two of them apart. He noticed she was wearing a silver ornament in her hair, while Maudie was wearing a green one, and filed the fact firmly in his mind with a view to getting through the rest of the evening without making an awkward blunder.

The night passed most pleasantly. The music was entertaining and the refreshments were plentiful—rather too plentiful for Freddy, whose ability to resist the next cocktail was always inversely proportional to the number of drinks he had already consumed. At some point in the proceedings he was hazily aware of being seized by Minnie and Maudie and hauled across the room towards someone brandishing a camera.

'Smile,' said the photographer.

Freddy grinned idiotically as the twins draped themselves over him and each planted a kiss on him at once, one on each cheek. A blinding flash went off. As Freddy's eyesight slowly returned a figure standing before him came gradually into focus. Its voice was familiar.

'I expect this is all for the paper, is it?' said Gertie. 'A bit of colour for this long story you're writing, yes?'

'Oh—ah,' said Freddy as the twins melted away. 'Hallo, Gertie. I didn't know you were going to be here.'

'That's obvious enough,' she replied. She was looking at him oddly. Freddy glanced down and found he was wearing a grass skirt and a garland of imitation flowers around his neck. He had no idea how or when they had got there.

'Well, I'm pleased to see you're having fun,' she said.

Freddy noticed a young man he knew slightly hovering a few yards away, watching the exchange and eyeing Gertie with interest.

'Why are you here with old Biffy Burfoot?' he asked.

'He's staying with us for a few weeks while Father tries to get him a job at the Foreign Office,' replied Gertie. 'He wanted to come out this evening, and since you'd ditched me I didn't have a good excuse to get out of it. I suspect Father has him in mind as a potential husband for me or possibly Clemmie.'

'Does he, now? Not exactly your type, I shouldn't have thought.'

'He's all right,' said Gertie, regarding young Biffy dispassionately. 'A trifle lacking in sparkle, perhaps, but one can at least be reasonably certain of never finding him wearing two chorus-girls and a hula-hula skirt when one runs across him unexpectedly in town. Some women look for that sort of thing in a man, oddly enough.'

'Don't tell me you've never done worse,' said Freddy, who was not too inebriated to put up a spirited defence. 'I've seen the photographs and haven't complained once.'

'Ha, yes, I am rather a terror, aren't I?' She glanced back at the young man. 'Listen, I've got to go, but I'll see you tomorrow. Don't forget. By the way, if you've any sense you'll stop drinking now, but I know you haven't, so at least try and remember your address for the taxi driver.'

And with that she was gone. Freddy was not certain whether he ought to feel disconcerted or not, but he had no time to ponder the question, for his services were required for dancing again. A few minutes later he saw Gertie and Biffy leaving, following which he proceeded to get thoroughly drunk, as she had predicted. At a certain point he found himself behaving disgracefully in a corner with Minnie. The cocktails must be his only excuse, for shamefully his chief concern was to make quite sure that Gertie had not returned unexpectedly and would not see him. Then he was dancing with Peggy again, and she was telling him something about Dinah, although he could not hear what. A little while later Minnie grabbed him again and pulled him back into the corner, although he was having great difficulty in remaining upright by this time. Further disgraceful conduct occurred.

'It's a good thing you're both wearing those head-dress things, or I shouldn't be able to tell you apart,' he slurred at last.

'There's only the one now—mine broke ten minutes ago, so I'm wearing Minnie's,' she replied.

'What?'

Freddy by now was not keeping up with anything but he sensed dimly that this was important information. She merely shook her head and gave him to understand through gestures that the music was too loud for conversation, and in any case she was more interested in other pursuits at present, so he put the matter to the back of his mind and very shortly forgot about it.

The next hour or so was a blur, but eventually Freddy became aware that people had begun singing *Show Me the Way to Go Home* and that the lights had gone on, and soon after that he found himself being escorted kindly but firmly from the premises. Despite Gertie's earlier misgivings, he made it into a taxi with some help from Trenton and one or two musicians, instructed the driver with the correct address, then on reaching home staggered into his flat and collapsed into bed.

Chapter Eleven

FREDDY WAS HALF-AWAKENED the next day by a sound which gradually intruded into his consciousness. At first he tried to ignore it, but it was continuous, insistent, seeming to say that it was determined to wake him up fully. At length he prised open his eyelids, which felt as though they had weights attached to them, and for some moments lay, blinking, with no idea where he was, since the room appeared unfamiliar to him. Gradually it came to him that he was lying the wrong way round on his bed, on top of the covers, with his feet on the pillow and his head half sliding off the foot. The stiff collar poking uncomfortably into his neck told him he was still fully dressed. This situation and manner of waking were not so rare for Freddy as to cause him any great degree of surprise or consternation. From long experience he knew he would in all likelihood spend the rest of the day alternating between periods of sleeping it off, and periods of wakefulness in which he would attempt to piece together the memory of what he had done the night before. He was fairly sure it was Sunday, so he had the whole day in which to recover—although to judge by the position of the sun, which was streaming directly onto him, since he had omitted to close the curtains, there was not much of the day left. Peering at his watch, he found it was close on three o'clock. He raised his head slowly, in some fear that his brain would dislodge itself if he moved too abruptly, groped for the blankets, and commenced the delicate operation to rearrange himself in the correct manner on the bed, in preparation for the nap he knew was necessary to enable him to keep down the hearty meal which would restore him to full vitality some time in the early evening, as per his usual routine.

But the noise had not gone away, and at last his brain registered what it was. Somebody was knocking at the door, seemingly without any intention of stopping. Freddy turned his head to listen—too quickly, for it disrupted the smooth running of the careful sequence of movements, and caused him to slide off the bed and land on the floor with a thump. Winded, he hauled himself to his feet and staggered to the front door. Squinting through the peep-hole he saw to his surprise one of the twins standing there. He had almost no memory of the night before, but vaguely remembered he had agreed to go to their birthday party. Presumably it had been a good one.

'Am I late?' she called through the door. Freddy opened it.

'So you are up. I thought you'd never answer,' she said, breezing past him into the flat. She looked very wide awake and in full possession of all her faculties. Freddy wondered if the party had indeed taken place, since to judge from her appearance she had partaken of a light supper after the performance of *Have At It!* the previous evening, gone to bed at a sensible hour, and sprung gaily out of bed early that morning for a session of vigorous callisthenics and a brisk stroll around the park.

'This is a smart place,' she observed, glancing around. 'Our digs aren't anywhere near so nice. The woman who runs the boarding-house is a bit of a tartar and keeps threatening to throw us out, so we have to climb in through a window if we stay out too late. You'd think she'd be used to theatrical people by now.'

She did not seem to have noticed the dishevelled state of him, or the fact that he was still wearing a dinner-suit and a bow tie that was half-undone at three o'clock on a Sunday afternoon, and chattered on happily.

'I had the most awful trouble giving Maudie the slip. I didn't tell her we were meeting today, you see, so I had to wait until Mr. Ferretti—he's one of the other lodgers—had got her talking before I could sneak out. He's an awful old gossip, so I expect he kept her busy for a while.'

'Meeting—today?' managed Freddy, seizing on something solid among the barrage of speech. An awful feeling began to steal over him.

'She'll be ever so jealous. We get along famously in every-thing except men, you see,' she explained. 'In most things we're so alike you'd almost think we were the same person, but she can't bear it whenever I find a nice boy-friend. We've come almost to blows at times. There was one chap a couple of years ago—it was in Felixstowe, and he was playing the second lead in *Dance Until Dawn*. He was a darling, but Maudie wouldn't give us a moment to ourselves, so we had to sneak around and make sure she wasn't close by whenever we wanted to you know what, otherwise she'd make a terrible scene. But as it turned out he was already married and we ended up saying a tearful goodbye on the pier at Eastbourne.'

Freddy was racking his brains frantically, trying to remember what exactly had happened at the party. He vaguely recalled someone putting him in a grass skirt and taking his photograph, and Gertie had been there—yes, he was sure of that—but what had happened next? And what could have possessed him to invite Minnie to his flat?'

'At any rate, Maudie's not here now,' Minnie said, sidling

up to him. 'We're all alone.' She slid her arms about his neck and smiled winningly up at him.

'Er—' said Freddy, becoming really alarmed now. What exactly had he committed himself to? He was just wondering how to disentangle himself tactfully when to his relief there was another sharp rap at the door.

'Bother,' said Minnie, retreating slightly.

Hoping against hope it was not his mother, who would only complicate matters further, Freddy went to look through the peep-hole again and to his dismay saw Maudie. It was at that precise moment that memory flooded back like an unstoppable tide. All at once a complete picture of the events of the previous night presented itself before him, the significance of the broken head-dress was explained to him, and he became fully aware that he had unwittingly made an exhibition of himself at separate times with both twins at their own birthday party.

'It's me,' called Maudie gaily through the door. Minnie's eyes widened.

'Oh, goodness!' she exclaimed. 'How did she find us? You'll have to hide me or I'll never hear the end of it.'

Freddy looked about wildly. The last thing he wanted was two women making a scene in his flat at a moment when his capabilities were not at their most finely honed.

'In there!' he hissed, opening the bedroom door and gesticulating.

Minnie needed no further urging, and disappeared as the knocking became louder. Freddy went to answer the door. Maudie was standing there, looking just as fresh and well-rested as her sister. She came in without waiting to be invited.

'I thought for a second I'd got the wrong place,' she said cheerfully. 'You simply can't imagine how hard it was to get away from Minnie. I had to pretend I was going downstairs to talk to the old fellow on the first floor, or I do believe I'd never have managed to escape. She'd kick up an awful stink if she knew I was coming here. She's terribly jealous, you know, and it's almost impossible to be alone with a man when she's loitering around, glaring at us. I'm so glad we have this place to ourselves.' She threw off her hat, sat down on the sofa and patted the cushion next to her. 'Why don't we get cosy?' she suggested, eyeing him invitingly.

At any other time Freddy would almost certainly have had the ready wit to invent an excuse to get rid of both her and Minnie without too much harm done, but they had caught him by surprise and before his brain was up to full speed. He was casting desperately around for a good reason why she could not stay, when there was yet another knock on the door. With a mounting sense of foreboding he looked through the peep-hole, saw Gertie, and remembered too late that they had agreed to meet in Hyde Park at three and go for a walk. Had he not been in so much trouble he could almost have laughed at her perfect timing. Instead he suppressed a panicked groan.

'It's my sister!' he hissed urgently to Maudie, improvising rapidly as necessity jolted his brain sharply back into action. 'She mustn't see you here! She's planning to take her vows soon and join the Convent of the Holy Mother of St. Euphemius, and she objects on principle to mixed company. In any other circumstances I'd take my chances, but she's prone to fainting fits and if she finds I've been allowing young ladies to make free of the place there's more than a little likelihood that we'll have to spend the rest of the afternoon scraping her off the floor and plying her with brandy—which, incidentally, is a vice she has *no* objection to.'

'That's all right,' said Maudie, jumping up. 'I'll go in here and you get rid of her as soon as you can.' She made a dive for the bedroom as she spoke.

'No!' exclaimed Freddy, but it was too late, for she had already disappeared through the door.

'Let me in, you ass,' came Gertie's voice. 'I know you're in there.'

Hoping fervently that the twins would have the sense to keep their voices down and their row for later, Freddy opened the front door. Gertie entered.

'I *thought* three o'clock would be a safe enough time for an appointment, but given the state of you last night I suppose I ought to have known,' she said. 'Luckily I'd had the feeling this might happen, so I borrowed Selworthy and the Rolls rather than walking and came here once it became obvious you weren't going to turn up. Father doesn't need him for the rest of the afternoon and he won't mind sitting in the car with his *Sunday Herald* while I'm here.'

Since Freddy's main object at that moment was to get Gertie out of his flat as quickly as possible so that Minnie and Maudie could be discreetly removed without her discovering their presence, this would not do.

'I'm awfully sorry, Gertie—I got to bed later than I thought. But we can still go for a walk. Listen, why don't you go downstairs and wait in the car and I'll have a quick wash and change and join you in fifteen minutes.'

'I can just as well wait here. I don't suppose Selworthy has any delicate sensibilities we need worry about.' She turned to sit, then stopped short. 'Freddy, why is there a woman's hat on your sofa?' she asked in an even tone.

Before Freddy could reply she strode over to the bedroom door and flung it open, to surprised squeaks from Minnie and Maudie, who had been huddled together by the door listening shamelessly through the crack. A short silence descended as Gertie regarded Freddy quizzically. There was no choice but to brazen it out.

'Gertie, you remember Minnie and Maudie, don't you?' he said breezily. 'They're here to—er—'

There his inspiration deserted him, and another silence fell which threatened to lengthen into positive awkwardness. Fortunately—or perhaps unfortunately—just then there was another knock at the door. Gertie went to open it. It was Peggy.

'What are you doing here?' said Minnie and Maudie together, as Freddy closed his eyes and prayed for deliverance.

'I beg your pardon, I didn't mean to intrude,' began Peggy, looking from Gertie to Freddy, but at the twins' words she stopped.

'You two? Don't tell me you're up to your tricks again. I thought you'd stopped all that.'

Minnie and Maudie both began to reply at once, but Gertie now spoke up.

'It's quite obvious you're busy at the moment,' she said pointedly to Freddy. 'I did want to talk to you, but it'll have to wait now as Mother and I are off to Norfolk in a couple of hours.' She glanced at the other visitors. 'You seem to have a very full diary at the moment. Do let me know when you can fit me in, won't you?'

'Gertie—' began Freddy, but she had gone.

'Oops,' said one of the twins.

'That wasn't meant to happen,' said the other.

'Look, you two idiots,' said Peggy. 'I thought you'd given up all this tomfoolery.'

'We wouldn't have done it if he hadn't been so beautifully squiffy last night,' said Maudie. 'But it was such a prime opportunity we couldn't resist.'

'And Freddy can take a joke, can't you Freddy?' added Minnie.

'A joke?' said Freddy, staggered. 'Is that what this is meant to be?'

They hung their heads and made an unconvincing attempt to look ashamed.

'They used to do it all the time,' Peggy said. 'I lost count of the number of puzzled men who used to turn up at the stage door after one of their pranks. It was rather tedious.'

The twins pouted.

'No it wasn't, it was fun,' said Maudie. 'But after a while we got tired of it and stopped.'

'A good thing too,' said Peggy sharply. 'A joke's all very well, but you'll end up getting into trouble that way.'

'Well, of all the—' began Freddy, then stopped. He ought to have been highly indignant at having been hoodwinked in such a manner, but as a connoisseur of practical jokes himself he had to admit they had brought it off very professionally. 'Don't do it again, that's all.'

'Sorry, Freddy,' they chorused dutifully. 'You won't get into trouble, will you?' added Maudie. 'It was only meant as a bit of harmless fun. I hope your girl-friend isn't too cross. She took it rather well, I thought.'

'Yes, she did, didn't she?' replied Freddy, half to himself. He was slightly disconcerted at how calmly Gertie had taken his antics of recent days. In his not inconsiderable experience women tended to hold forth angrily and at length when they caught him in equivocal situations with rival members of the female sex, but she seemed almost uninterested.

'But why are you here, Peggy?' the twins wanted to know.

'I came to ask Freddy for help,' she answered. 'But as a matter of fact I'm glad you're here too. Have you seen Dinah at all?'

'No, why?'

'Because she's gone missing. I haven't seen her since we came offstage last night and I don't know where she is.'

The twins looked at one another.

'I didn't see her at the party, did you?'

'No.'

'I didn't see her either,' said Freddy. 'She wasn't there.'

'Perhaps she didn't feel well and went home after the show,' suggested Maudie.

Peggy shook her head.

'I went to her place and they haven't seen her since yesterday morning. Besides, she told me she was looking forward to the party. Did either of you see her leaving the theatre last night?'

Neither twin had seen her at all last night, it seemed.

'Where can she be?' said Minnie.

'I don't know,' replied Peggy, looking worried.

Chapter Twelve

THE SUN WAS SINKING below the horizon when the four of them arrived at the Jollity Theatre, and darkness was falling.

'I might have come alone,' said Peggy. 'But I don't know— I felt I needed some company in case—in case—' She did not finish.

The Jollity was locked and deserted on the day of rest, but Peggy had managed to procure a key and they went in through the stage door. Not even Alf was at his post when they entered, and the place was in darkness.

'I don't like it,' said Minnie fearfully.

Peggy found a switch and the place was suddenly flooded with light.

'There,' she said. 'Let's go together.'

On the wall in Alf's box was a cabinet hung with the keys to all the dressing-rooms. The ones on the nearest corridor were very quickly run through, but there was no sign of Dinah.

'I don't believe she's here at all,' said Maudie. 'She probably decided to go somewhere else instead of our party.'

'No she didn't,' said Peggy from the doorway of their dressing-room. 'She left her coat, look.'

She indicated the article in question, which was hanging on a rail by Dinah's chair.

'Perhaps she brought another one for the party,' suggested Minnie, although without much conviction.

Freddy's senses were starting to tingle and he shook his head soberly. He did not like this at all. He proceeded along to the end of the passage and slowly mounted the steps to the dark corridor that ran behind the stage. It was the oddest feeling, but despite the silence he was almost sure somebody was here in the theatre with them.

'What can you see?' whispered Minnie from behind him. 'Is the ghost there?'

'Don't be silly,' he replied. 'I wish I had a torch, though. Do you know where the light switches are for this corridor?'

'Just a second,' came Peggy's voice. There was a click and the lights came on. The twins made sounds of relief.

'That's better. It doesn't look so frightening now, does it?' said Maudie.

Freddy made no reply. He looked into the unfinished dressing-room that had previously been home to the chorus, then glanced into the new lavatory, but saw nothing. He emerged and walked slowly along the corridor, looking into each room as he did so. Peggy, Minnie and Maudie hung back nervously, staying close to the steps and to each other.

'Anything?' asked Peggy.

'No.'

The door to the props room was slightly ajar, and Freddy pushed at it. It swung open with an ominous creak.

'Someone ought to put some oil on that hinge,' he remarked.

He took a step into the room. Odd-shaped shadows loomed out of the darkness towards him. He groped for the light switch, and suddenly the shapes were revealed as the ordinary, everyday articles he had seen the other day. He scanned the room slowly. Everything seemed normal. He picked his way through the various objects, turning his head this way and that, but saw nothing untoward.

'This place could do with tidying up,' said Peggy behind him, wrinkling her nose in the doorway.

Freddy retreated towards the door.

'Nothing here that I can see,' he said. He was about to put out the light when something caught his eye and he stopped. It was the steamer trunk from Loveday's dressing-room.

'Funny,' he said. 'I'm sure that trunk was standing on its end the other day. Who laid it down like that?'

He approached and bent to examine it. The trunk was fastened with a complicated array of catches, and he released them one by one and raised the lid.

'Damn,' he said softly as Peggy screamed.

Dinah was curled up inside almost as though she were asleep, her fluffy blonde hair spilling over her face and her hands. She was dressed in a pink satin evening-frock and matching shoes. There was no doubt at all that she was dead.

Peggy's scream had brought the twins running.

'Oh, *no!*' they cried together as they caught sight of the trunk and its terrible contents.

Peggy was looking at the scene through her fingers.

'But how did it happen?' she said.

'I don't know,' said Freddy grimly. 'But I'll tell you one thing—this isn't the work of a ghost. If I'm not much mistaken, she's been strangled.'

He stood up. Minnie and Maudie started to cry.

'So this is why she didn't come to our party. Oh, Dinah!'

Peggy was also fighting back tears.

'We can't leave her shoved in there like a pile of old clothes,' she said shakily as Freddy stood up and indicated that they were all to leave the room. 'Can't we get her out?'

'We mustn't touch anything,' he replied. 'The police will want to look at it. Come away now—there's nothing we can do for her.'

They went and telephoned the police immediately, then Freddy called Jenny too, and they went to wait in the stage door entrance lobby. The police duly arrived, followed shortly by Alf, who had presumably been summoned by Jenny.

''Ere, what's all this?' he demanded, at the sight of members of the constabulary tramping to and fro in his theatre.

In tearful confusion the girls explained the situation to him and his face darkened.

'There's no call for that,' was all he said. He stamped off along the corridor, most likely to get in the way of the police in the execution of their duty.

'When can we go home?' whimpered Maudie.

Freddy sought out a policeman and obtained his permission to send the girls away, since there was nothing they could do at present. A constable took their names and addresses and they departed soberly, but Freddy hung about in his capacity as a member of the press, for he knew this would be a big story, although he felt no pleasure in getting the scoop on his fellow reporters. In fact he was furious with himself for having allowed this to happen. He had known Dinah was keeping some secret from him, but it had slipped his memory and he had neglected to urge her on the matter. If he had only spoken to her again he might have found out what it was she had been hiding, and she might still have been alive, for he was sure that her death was connected in some way to whatever it was she had known. Remembering the little scene outside the restaurant the other day, it then occurred to him that Peggy at least was almost certainly privy to the same information. It was too late to ask her about it, for she had gone home now, but he would speak to her as soon as he could and find out what it was that Dinah had hidden from him.

A familiar voice interrupted his ruminations.

'What are you doing here? No press allowed,' it snapped.

'Inspector Entwistle,' said Freddy, looking up. 'Fancy

seeing you here. Have they just called you in? I trust you're well.'

'Never mind that,' said Entwistle, who was a good man, although a little on the gruff side and afflicted with a general dislike of the press. 'Off with you. You'll get all the details in good time.'

'As a matter of fact I'm the one who discovered the body, so I'm afraid you're stuck with me for the present.'

'Is that so?' Entwistle regarded him narrowly, disappeared along the corridor apparently to consult with his colleagues and find out whether Freddy was telling the truth, and returned a few minutes later. 'So then, you're the one who found this—' he glanced down at his notebook '—Dinah Belmonte, are you? May I ask why you were wandering around an empty theatre on a Sunday, and why you opened the trunk?'

'I didn't just turn up here for the fun of it. A friend of Dinah's was worried about her as she'd gone missing and nobody saw her leave the theatre last night. I noticed the trunk had been moved since I last saw it the other day so I opened it, that's all.'

'Did you have any particular reason to think she was dead?'

'Not especially, but I've a cynical, suspicious turn of mind so I did wonder. She didn't turn up to a party, you see, and her friends and I were concerned about her so I thought it couldn't do any harm to scout about here a little. One or two odd things have happened here lately, and I've been looking into them.'

'What sort of odd things?'

'Well, the producer of the show and another chorus-girl both died here recently in somewhat vague circumstances, although neither of the deaths was put down to foul play.'

He gave the inspector a brief summary of his investigation into the deaths of Septimus Gooch and Una Bryant.

'Hmm, yes, I remember reading about them in the paper,' commented Entwistle, making a note. 'I'll have to take a look at the reports. So you say you hadn't found out anything?'

'The theatre-folk have been talking of a ghost, but of course that's nonsense. Ghosts don't kill people as a rule—or at least, they certainly don't strangle them and shove them in a trunk.'

'Not in my experience,' agreed Entwistle. 'Stay here a minute, won't you?'

He went off, leaving Freddy to kick his heels impatiently, for he would rather have been watching the police at work. A short while later Sergeant Bird arrived. He was less morose than his superior and inclined to view Freddy more leniently.

'Hallo, Freddy, what are you doing here?' he asked.

Freddy explained.

'Chorus-girls, eh? I wouldn't have had you down as a— what do they call it? A stage door johnny.'

'I'm no such thing,' replied Freddy with dignity.

The sergeant winked jovially and went off, and Freddy was once more left alone in the lobby. He dug in his pocket for his notebook and began composing a story, intending to stop at the offices of the *Clarion* on the way home and have it put in the morning edition. He finished then rose to go and see what the police were doing, since everyone seemed to have forgotten him completely. Just then Jenny arrived in a hurry.

'Is it true?' she demanded breathlessly when she saw him. 'Oh, Freddy, how could it have happened? Do you think it's—'

'Do I think it's connected with the other things? I don't see how it can't be,' replied Freddy. 'But equally I don't see where it fits in.'

'Poor Dinah. Where is she now?'

'In the props room.'

They went together and found the police busy with their work while Alf sparred with a constable, who was attempting patiently to get information out of him as to the practical arrangements in the theatre.

'We did have a night-watchman here a until a few months ago,' said Jenny in reply to one of the questions, since Alf was being his usual cryptic self. 'But he went and we hadn't replaced him yet.'

'Surely she died not long after the show, though,' Freddy observed. 'The place can't have been long deserted, otherwise Dinah wouldn't have been here, as she was expected at a birthday party.'

'That's as may be,' the constable conceded, 'but we must ascertain all the facts.'

'Might I ask who you are?' inquired Inspector Entwistle, coming out of the props room and catching sight of Jenny.

'I'm Jenny Minter, and I suppose I own this theatre—or I will once everything is settled. I expect you have some questions for me, don't you?'

They stepped to one side and entered into conversation. Freddy hung back and attempted to fade into the background since he wanted to observe proceedings without being thrown out.

'Look at this,' someone called from the props room. 'Someone's been sleeping in here.'

'What?' said Entwistle. He left Jenny and went to where the man was indicating. Freddy followed. A Japanese painted screen stood across one corner of the room. He had noticed it the other day, but saw now what he had not seen before, which was that it had been placed across a sort of deep alcove so as to hide it completely. Behind it was a regular little nest. Several cushions had been arranged on the floor as a makeshift mattress, with some rugs as bed-covers.

'What do we have here, then? Do you know anything about it?' Entwistle asked Jenny.

'Not a thing,' she replied in surprise. 'I haven't been into this corner in ages. As a matter of fact I'd forgotten it was here.'

'It looks like it's been recently occupied,' observed Freddy.

Entwistle glanced at him impatiently.

'I thought I told you to wait out there. I'll see to you in good time.'

Freddy grimaced at his own carelessness and retreated into the corridor. Entwistle seemed determined to keep him waiting. He looked at his watch, wondering when he would be able to leave, for he had not eaten that day, and just at that moment caught a movement out of the corner of his eye. He turned his head sharply. At the far end of the corridor a man stood stock still, having apparently been interrupted in the act of creeping towards the props room by the realization that the place was full of people. As Freddy looked up he turned and made a bolt for it.

'Hi!' exclaimed Freddy and gave chase, joined by a constable. Their quarry was not very fast and he suffered from a limp, but he had a good head start and they did not catch up with him until he was halfway across the workshop near the loading entrance.

'You let me alone!' he gasped, as they caught hold of him. He did not seem in a condition to put up much of a fight, and indeed the brief chase appeared to have thoroughly exhausted him.

'Who have we got here?' said Sergeant Bird, coming up.

Freddy thought he looked familiar, but could not immediately place him. The man looked sulky and said nothing, and Freddy was visited by a sudden remembrance.

'I know you—you're Bert Spooner!' he said.

Chapter Thirteen

'I DON'T KNOW why you need so many coppers to arrest one man for trespassing,' grumbled Bert Spooner, the taller, thinner half of Jinks and Spooner. 'Besides, I haven't done any harm. All I wanted was a place to sleep after that old devil Septimus Gooch gave me the chuck. I didn't have a penny to my name and I couldn't work because nobody wants half a double act, and he wouldn't let Morry out of his contract until the end of the run, so what choice did I have?'

'How long have you been sleeping here,' asked Jenny in astonishment.

'Matter of a month or two. Maybe since the end of August.'

'All this time? Oh, Bert,' said Jenny with pity. 'Why didn't you say something? We'd have found a place for you. I know Septimus was a little harsh on you, but you could have come and spoken to me. Or if you didn't want to do that you could have come out after he died, at least.'

'Well I'd got comfortable, hadn't I? Better this place than some poky attic with no hot water at a guinea a week. It's warm here, and free. I wasn't going to stay much longer— Morry said you were inclined to let him out of the contract, and all we had to do was wait until he'd collected the money together to get us across to New York, so I thought there was no harm in staying for another few weeks.'

'You've been sleeping in the dressing-rooms, haven't you?' said Freddy suddenly.

'I took a key once or twice, when the floor got too much for my rheumatism,' he admitted. 'Those cushions are soft enough when you first lie down on 'em, but by the morning it's like lying on bare boards.'

'So it was you moving people's things.'

'Did I? I dare say I shifted some bits and pieces off a couch or two to make room,' he said. 'But I never took anything.'

'Did you stay in the theatre all the time?'

'No, mostly I'd be out during the daytime, but I feel the cold at this time of year and sometimes my leg would be paining me so much by the end of the day I'd come back just for the warmth. I tried my best to stay hidden, though. I knew they hadn't finished the works here so there was a fair chance nobody would come up to this corridor and see me and take fright.'

'You were seen by one or two people, as a matter of fact,' said Freddy. 'They thought you were a ghost.'

'Did they, now?' Spooner seemed surprised.

'Yes, they described a tall, thin man with a limp, covered in dust and groaning.'

'The rheumatism's a sore trial sometimes. And I dare say it is a bit dusty in that corner,' he conceded. 'I don't always get a chance to look in a glass and smarten up.' He let out a hoarse laugh. 'A ghost, eh? That's a new one on me.'

'You knew he was here, didn't you, Alf?' said Freddy.

The stage door-keeper pursed up his lips and eyed Jenny Minter sideways.

'No harm in it, was there, Jen?'

'It's a bit late to be asking that now, but I don't suppose so,' she replied resignedly.

'Where were you last night?' Inspector Entwistle asked.

'Here. Well, not all night,' replied Spooner. 'Morry subbed me and I went and had a bite to eat then spent the rest of the evening in the Crown and Anchor.'

'And what time did you return?'

'Half past eleven or thereabouts, it must have been. I loitered a bit on the way back until I thought most of 'em would have gone home, then came in through the back door here so as not to be noticed.'

'You have a key?'

Spooner indicated that that was the case, although he refused to be drawn on where he had got it. Freddy suspected that either Alf or Morry Jinks had passed him a copy and he did not wish to get them into trouble.

'Look, why are you asking me all these questions?' Spooner went on. 'I've told you what I've been doing. I've kept myself to myself and haven't half-inched anything. Now, if you're going to charge me with trespass I'd be obliged if you'd get on with it, so I can go and find myself a place to stay before everything closes for the night.'

'Not so fast,' said Entwistle. 'We haven't finished yet, not by a long way. I'd like to know whether you saw Dinah Belmonte yesterday evening.'

'Dinah who?'

'She was one of the chorus-dancers.'

'I never saw any chorus-dancers yesterday. What has this Dinah Belmonte got do to with anything?'

'She was found strangled not ten feet from that cosy nook of yours not two hours ago,' replied Inspector Entwistle deliberately.

If Bert Spooner was guilty he did a very good job of disguising it. His mouth dropped open and he glanced towards the door of the props room, seeming for the first time to become aware of the activity that was going on inside.

'What? In there, you mean? That's impossible!'

'Where were you just now?'

'I nipped out for a couple of hours, just to get some fags and a breath of fresh air. Do you mean someone did her in while I was out?'

'No, she's most likely been dead since last night,' answered Entwistle.

'No she hasn't, or I'd have seen her. My eyesight's not what it was but don't tell me I wouldn't have spotted a corpse lying about in the props room, 'cause I'm not that blind.'

'She was found in a trunk.'

'Well I never saw her, and I swear I never touched her, if that's what you're driving at.'

'That remains to be seen,' said Entwistle non-committally. 'Was anyone in the theatre when you returned last night?'

'Not as far as I know. It was quiet enough so I assumed they'd all gone home, or to wherever it is they all go of a Saturday night.'

'And you're certain you didn't see Miss Belmonte? She didn't find you here and threaten to tell Miss Minter you were sleeping here on the sly, for example?'

'No!'

'Hmm.' Entwistle glanced at his watch. 'We've still a lot to do here, but we'll need you to come to the station and answer some more questions. P. C. Lamb will take you.'

'What? There's no call for that! I told you I had nothing to do with all this.'

'Then you've nothing to worry about, have you? If you're innocent then we'll find it out as soon as may be. But it's getting late, you can't stay here, and we'll want to speak to you again tomorrow. Besides, I'd have thought you'd be all for a square meal or two and a night in a proper bed for once.'

'Well, yes, but not in the clink!' exclaimed the comedian.

'Where's Morry? Who's going to tell him?'

'I'm sure this will all be straightened out tomorrow,' said Jenny. 'I'll let Morry know what's happened.'

Bert Spooner was borne away protesting, and Entwistle returned to his work.

The police presumably knew what they were doing, but still Freddy was not satisfied. Inspector Entwistle seemed to be of the opinion that Dinah had discovered Spooner's presence the previous night and that he had strangled her to stop her talking, but it seemed highly unlikely to Freddy. Spooner would not have got into very much trouble had it been known he had been staying at the theatre—Jenny's reaction on finding out about it made that perfectly obvious—so why on earth should he have committed murder to keep the fact quiet? And why should he have concealed Dinah's body so close to his own hiding-place? The Jollity had been empty for the whole of Saturday night and Sunday, and although it was situated in one of the busiest streets in Piccadilly, there was a network of quiet alleys and yards at the rear of the building that would be deserted very early on a Sunday morning. Why, he might easily have taken her body out in the dark and concealed it somewhere outside, so that when she was found it would be thought that she had been attacked by a stranger. Why should he have hidden her in the steamer trunk?

Somewhere nearby Inspector Entwistle was questioning Alf, whose chief concern was apparently to make it clear to everybody that none of this was his fault. He had seen nothing and done nothing except his duty as an employee of the Jollity Theatre. As far as he knew all the girls had left at about half past ten to go to a party. Some of the orchestra had gone to the party too, he thought, but he could not say with any certainty at what time they had left, because their room was around the other side and they generally went out through a different door. As for the rest, Miss Curtis and her dresser had gone shortly after the show ended, followed soon afterwards by Artie Jennings, Mr. Bagshawe and Morry Jinks, while Miss Oliver had gone out with Jenny. Mr. St. Clair had left and then returned for something he had forgotten, then Alf himself had locked up and been out of the place by just after eleven. No, he had not seen Bert Spooner or Dinah Belmonte. He knew Spooner had been living there but had left him to it and not interfered. Out of sight, out of mind, was his motto. Jen was a good girl and he knew she wouldn't make a fuss if it all came out. That was his story and he would not be budged on it.

'We'll need to question the cast and the orchestra tomorrow morning, and find out their movements,' Inspector Entwistle said to Jenny. 'Can you get them all here, do you think?'

'I'll see what I can do,' she replied.

'Now, I'd just like you to put me clear on one or two things,' said Entwistle. The two of them went off, leaving Freddy alone in the stage door corridor, frowning to himself. He drifted into the room that was usually occupied by Peggy, the twins and Dinah. It was strewn with discarded clothes, bottles of cosmetics and other feminine sundries, and looked as though it must be very cramped when they were all in there together. Dinah's coat was still hanging on the rail, and he looked quickly through the pockets but found nothing. She had kept her tiny section of the room very neat, arranging her make-up in tidy rows. A sensational magazine was lying on her chair where she had presumably left it, and he glanced at it then threw it down again. There seemed nothing to be learned here, so he went out.

Diagonally opposite was Loveday's room. Freddy went in, trying to call to memory the night when Septimus Gooch had died. Was there any connection between the three deaths? Had there been only Septimus and Una Bryant to consider the answer might easily have been no, but Dinah's murder could not be a coincidence, surely? Freddy shook his head. He was as sure as he could be that Dinah had known or suspected something about the two deaths and had died for it.

He looked around in case anything should strike him that he had not thought of before. There was the comfortable sofa on which Bert Spooner had occasionally slept, moving Loveday's things out of the way first and thus giving rise to the rumour of a ghost. He stared at it absently for a few moments, wondering whether Spooner knew anything about Una or Septimus, then decided it was really time to leave, since the police were obviously busy at present and he would have to get to the *Clarion*'s offices soon if he wanted to catch the morning edition. He was about to go and find Jenny to tell her so, when he heard her somewhere nearby, talking to Entwistle.

'…no, this wasn't finished. There was some disagreement with the builders when my husband was alive, but I plan to finish the works as soon as possible. These rooms are much more spacious as you can see…'

Freddy went out into the corridor, but to his surprise Jenny was not there. He glanced into the nearest dressing-rooms but she was nowhere to be seen—nor was she in any of the rooms on the stage door corridor, or in the wings by the stage, or in the lobby. He went up to the corridor behind the stage, heard Jenny's voice again and saw her standing with Entwistle just outside the door of the out-of-bounds lavatory which led off the room the chorus had formerly occupied.

Puzzled, he returned to Loveday's dressing-room. Now he could hear Inspector Entwistle, more faintly this time, asking some question about the various entrances to the theatre. His voice was clear, and yet Entwistle was in a room on a different corridor more than twenty feet away and around a corner. Freddy listened for the source of the sound. It seemed to be coming from somewhere near the wash-basin. He went towards it and listened for several moments, and suddenly he understood. His brow cleared.

'Well, I'll be damned,' he murmured.

Chapter Fourteen

'I WANT a word with you about Una,' Freddy said in a low voice to Peggy the next day.

He had found the girls on the stage of the Jollity with the other cast members and the orchestra, as the police called everybody one by one to question them as to their movements on Saturday night. There was no matinée that day, and it was still doubtful as to whether the evening performance would be able to go ahead, although Jenny could not see why not, and had told the police so. They would let her know by lunchtime, she said. In the meantime, the chorus would have to manage with one less member until they could find someone to replace Dinah. Peggy, Minnie and Maudie had just finished speaking to the police and were standing in a huddle, away from everyone else.

'What is it?' asked Peggy, a wary expression crossing her face.

'Not here. Somewhere private.'

She glanced at Minnie and Maudie.

'If it's about Una you'd better come too.'

They obtained permission to leave and went in search of a

place to talk. In the end they found a nearby public gardens and sat down.

'Well?' said Peggy. 'What is it you want?'

'I want you to come clean about how Una died,' replied Freddy. 'I know you know what happened.'

'We don't, I promise you,' she insisted in surprise, as the twins shook their heads in agreement. 'I wish we did.'

'But you haven't told me everything.'

'What makes you think that?'

'Because I know about the voices. They were yours, weren't they?'

The twins gasped.

'How do you know?' they said together, as Peggy glared at them.

'An accident, followed by a bit of deduction,' he replied. 'I found out by chance last night that voices carry clearly along the new water pipes in the out-of-bounds cloak-room to a pipe near the wash-basin in Loveday's dressing-room, and as far as I knew you were the only ones using that cloak-room. You wanted to play a prank on Loveday, so you took it in turns to go into the ladies' and whisper down the pipe while one or other of you stood guard outside her dressing-room to make sure nobody else went in while you were doing it, because you didn't want anybody else to hear.'

They all looked at one another.

'Rumbled!' exclaimed Maudie tragically.

Minnie giggled.

'It was such a beautiful trick. She thought she was going out of her mind. And it served her right. We discovered how it worked by accident, and then Maudie had the idea.'

'One of my better ones, if I say so myself,' said Maudie. 'Loveday's quite insufferable, and we'd been looking for a way to pay her back after what she did to Peggy, who's a darling. There didn't seem any harm in it, and it was fun to hear

Loveday shriek. We didn't mean anything bad to happen, though.'

'Where did Una come in?' asked Freddy.

'She did the best voices,' answered Peggy.

'She used to impersonate Loveday,' added Maudie. 'You know, when she's having one of her sulks. You should have heard it—I couldn't have told the difference. It used to make us howl with laughter.'

'It drove Loveday mad,' said Minnie.

'Was Una the only one who did it?' inquired Freddy.

'No, we all took turns,' replied Peggy. 'We didn't want to look suspicious, you see. One of us would go into the W. C. and whisper while another would stand just outside at the top of the steps watching for anyone coming, and a third would stand outside Loveday's door ready to give a warning if anybody else turned up.'

'It was a jolly good laugh,' said Minnie. Her brow wrinkled. 'That is, until Una died. We stopped after that, because it wasn't funny any more.'

'What happened?'

'She wasn't supposed to do it alone, because as we told you we needed someone to keep watch so as not to get caught,' answered Peggy. 'But once or twice she got a bit carried away and did it anyway. I think that's what she'd been doing that night. She did it alone just before the show, and I guess she'd decided to do it again in the interval. She didn't come on stage in the second act, and we were worried, so we went back and looked for her while all the others were taking their bows.'

'But you didn't find her in the dressing-room as you said, did you?' said Freddy.

It had been half a guess, but their guilty expressions told him immediately that he had hit the mark.

'No. She was in the cloak-room,' said Peggy reluctantly.

'And you moved her body.'

'What were we supposed to do?' demanded Maudie. 'If

they'd found her dead in the ladies' the game would have been up. We weren't meant to use the place anyway, and if they'd figured out what we were up to we'd have been in the most awful trouble. Loveday would have had old Gooch sack us for sure. We didn't have much time to think, but we knew we had to get her out of there sharp because we only had a minute or two before the rest of the cast came offstage, so we carried her to the dressing-room, then raised the alarm.'

'We thought she'd been taken by a sudden illness,' said Peggy. 'But Loveday kicked up an awful fuss and started saying it was a ghost, which of course it wasn't, because *we* were the ghost—the one she was talking about, at any rate. Then someone got hold of the old story about the theatre's being haunted and half the chorus claimed they'd seen mysterious figures wandering around—although it was obviously all in their imagination, because if they'd really seen something one of them surely would have realized it was only Bert Spooner. I'd have realized it myself but I'm short-sighted and didn't see him properly, and Dinah only didn't twig because she didn't join the chorus until after Bert had been sacked so didn't know him. But then Loveday started blathering about ghosts at the inquest and it all got very silly.'

'That's why we got hold of you,' said Minnie to Freddy. 'You turned up and started asking whether we'd seen anything, and Morry said you were there because of Jenny, so we thought perhaps she suspected what we'd been up to and was trying to catch us out. We wanted to know what Jenny knew. Dinah was starting to believe there really was a ghost, you see, because of seeing Bert, and we were worried she might blurt the whole thing out one day, so we were hoping you'd prove the ghost wasn't real. And we really did want to know how Una died, because we were worried it might have been our fault somehow.'

'Did Dinah take part in the trick?' Freddy asked.

'Sometimes. Not as often as we did,' answered Maudie.

'I'm not proud of what we did to Una, you know,' Peggy said uncomfortably. 'It was an awful, cowardly thing to do. That's why I was hoping the inquest would show she'd died of something quite natural. She'd been sickly as a child, you see. If it had been something like that then it wouldn't really have mattered that we'd moved her—or that's what I told myself, anyhow. But they couldn't say what killed her, and that's when we started wondering whether it was all our fault. Perhaps all the sneaking around was too much for her, and caused her heart to fail, or something of the kind. I was hoping you'd find out it had nothing to do with us. I'd never have forgiven myself if she'd died because of us and we'd made it impossible to identify a cause of death just because we wanted to get ourselves out of trouble.'

Freddy could not think of anything to say that would give her comfort, because that was exactly what they might have done, and it was too late now to put things right.

'Do you think there's a connection between what happened to Una and what happened to Dinah?' asked Minnie.

'Yes, I rather think there is,' answered Freddy.

'They're saying Bert killed Dinah,' said Peggy. 'Is that true?'

'I don't know. They've arrested him, but I think it's just for the sake of keeping an eye on him for now. I can't see what motive he had, unless he also killed Una and Dinah knew it.'

'But Una wasn't murdered, was she?' she asked in horror.

'I don't know. I've no idea how she died. But I very much doubt Spooner had anything to do with either death.'

'But *someone* must have killed Dinah. What if there's a madman on the loose, killing chorus-girls? What if we're all in danger?' said Maudie.

They looked at one another, worried.

'I don't think this is the work of a madman,' said Freddy. 'I think Dinah knew or suspected something that would have got somebody into trouble if she'd mentioned it. I don't suppose she said anything to you?' He turned to Peggy. 'I heard you giving her a warning that day we had lunch.'

'Yes—I reminded her not to tell you about our moving Una, because I thought she might blab.'

'Was that the only thing? There wasn't anything else you wanted her to keep quiet about?'

'No, nothing at all. I promise you if we knew anything we'd say,' replied Peggy. 'A joke's one thing, but murder isn't funny.'

The twins nodded in agreement. They all seemed sincere enough.

Freddy was becoming more and more perplexed. The discovery of the girls' joke ought to have cleared things up somewhat, but instead it seemed to have made things even more complicated. The ghost—both ghosts, in fact—had been laid to rest now, but there was still no explanation for the events of recent months. Perhaps Septimus and Una had both died naturally in two quite unconnected incidents, but it was looking increasingly unlikely now that they had a third body on their hands. One thing that was certain was that Dinah Belmonte had been murdered—partly, he felt, through his own carelessness—and to make up for that he would do everything in his power to find out what had happened and who had killed her.

Chapter Fifteen

TUESDAY FOUND Freddy at Scotland Yard, where he had been summoned peremptorily by Inspector Entwistle. To his surprise he discovered that he was not to be shouted at, but rather that Entwistle wanted to pick his brains about the case since he had been in on it from the beginning. It seemed that after questioning Bert Spooner at length, the police had been forced to release him. Entwistle admitted that the case against him was not especially strong, since there was a good chance that Spooner had not even been in the theatre at the time Dinah was killed—which they had established as most likely between a quarter past ten, when she had last been seen, and about eleven o'clock, when everybody was thought to have gone home and Alf had locked up. According to Spooner himself, he had not returned to the Jollity until half past eleven, by which time Dinah was almost certainly already dead and in the trunk.

'The evidence is thin against him,' said Entwistle. 'In fact, the only thing we've got on him is that he was sleeping in the room where Dinah was found. He *might* have done it, but we'll never be able to make a case on that basis.'

'Were there any finger-prints on the steamer trunk catch-es?' asked Freddy.

'Only yours.'

Freddy grimaced.

'Ah. Of course. I must have wiped any others off when I opened it. That's a pity. Any prints elsewhere on the trunk, then?'

'Everyone's finger-prints and hand-prints were all over the thing, inside and out. It seems it was moved around the place regularly.'

'I think it was. As a matter of fact, it was in Loveday's room on the night Septimus died,' said Freddy. 'It's handy if one's short of space to put things. I say, though, I'm rather surprised you didn't think I'd done it. After all, I did turn up very conveniently and go straight to the hiding-place.'

'Well, naturally we looked into that,' replied Entwistle. 'But fortunately for you your alibi holds together. It seems you were one of a rowdy crowd drawing attention to yourselves at the Café Royal between nine o'clock and eleven or so. Once they'd finally persuaded you to leave you were seen getting into a taxi. You arrived at the Copernicus Club at ten past eleven or thereabouts and stayed there with a large party until you were all thrown out at four o'clock. You didn't have time to stop at the Jollity Theatre on the way and kill anyone.'

'You have been thorough. Well, now you know I'm not a murderer, how can I help? And if Spooner didn't kill Dinah, then who did?'

'That is the question, and I wanted to hear your view on the matter. If you want my opinion I think sooner or later we'll find out that Spooner *did* do it, but there are one or two things that don't tally, and it's only right that we look into every possibility.'

'What is it that doesn't tally?'

'Well, Spooner says he spent the evening at the Crown and

Anchor on Rathbone Place and got back to the Jollity at half past eleven, loitering on the way. We've spoken to the landlord, who says Spooner was inclined to linger over his last pint but was eventually booted out at five to eleven. It's a fifteen minute brisk walk so even if he was lying about having dawdled on the way, the soonest he could have got back to the Jollity was ten past eleven—and that's generous, what with that rheumatism of his. The question is: why would Dinah still be at the Jollity at that time, when the place had been locked up by then?'

'Perhaps she'd discovered earlier that Spooner was sleeping there and hung around waiting for him to return so she could confront him,' suggested Freddy.

'But she had a party to go to. Surely it wasn't so urgent that it couldn't have waited?'

'True. It's not exactly a convincing reason, is it? By the way, I imagine you're looking for a man? I mean, a woman couldn't have done it?'

'It would have to have been a very strong woman, to have got the better of a fit and healthy dancer.'

'Let's assume it was a man then. What do you think happened? What do you suppose led up to the murder?'

Entwistle consulted his notes.

'By all accounts Dinah was looking forward to the party at the Copernicus Club and was talking as though she planned to go. A couple of the girls say she changed into her evening-things quickly and left the room, and they don't remember seeing her after that.'

'Presumably she went to talk to someone, and the conversation ended in murder. But whom did she speak to?'

'And why should she have gone into that corridor at all if not to speak to Spooner? There must be some reason. I understand from Miss Minter that the rooms there were not supposed to be used.'

'They weren't supposed to be, no, but I know at least some of the chorus, including Dinah, had been using the lavatory that leads off their old dressing-room on the sly,' said Freddy. 'She might easily have gone up there for perfectly natural reasons.'

He did not mention the moving of Una Bryant's body for the present, as he was not sure what bearing it had on Dinah's death, and he did not want to get the girls into trouble if he could help it.

'Do we know for certain she died on the back corridor, by the way?' he went on.

'It seems most likely,' said Entwistle. 'If we assume she was killed during the period when everyone was changing to go home, it would be difficult for our murderer to do it on the stage door corridor without someone seeing him. It would make more sense for him to have done it at the back of the stage, which was mostly deserted. But what you say explains why Dinah might have been in that corridor. Perhaps she spotted Spooner when she went up there to powder her nose and asked him what he thought he was doing.'

'You think he got the wind up and strangled her in a panic? Is that it?'

'It's the best theory we have so far, although I admit it isn't a very satisfactory one.'

'What about alibis?' asked Freddy. 'Leaving aside motive, who had the opportunity to do it, apart from Spooner?'

Entwistle consulted his notes again.

'The orchestra all vouch for each other. It seems they left in a body as soon as the show had finished and went straight to the Copernicus Club. The movements of all the stage-hands have also been accounted for as far as we can tell. That leaves the cast and the stage-manager. Artie Jennings says he went straight home, and his wife and daughters confirm that. Morry Jinks also claims to have gone home, and his landlady agrees. We don't know whether either of them sneaked off and killed Dinah before they left, however. The same goes for Rupert St. Clair, who left then came back for his cane, and

Trenton Bagshawe, who says he went directly to the Copernicus Club. I understand Bagshawe is a friend of yours.'

'More or less. I was at school with his brother and friendly with his sister at one time. I can't see what possible motive he could have had for murder, as he's currently ga-ga over Miss Oliver. And I'd be astonished to find St. Clair had any interest in forcing his attentions onto young ladies. But that's assuming one particular motive. I take it Dinah wasn't interfered with at all?'

'No. That sort of crime we can understand, but this sort is a facer, when there's no obvious motive.'

'What about Alf? He wanders around the Jollity quite freely. He might easily have done it—much more easily than anyone else, in fact, since he was the one who locked up.'

'He might, yes, but again we have the question of motive. He might have had the opportunity, but so might any of them earlier on. As far as I can tell the place was in confusion immediately after the performance, and everybody was too occupied with their own business to pay much attention to what anybody else was doing. We don't think it was a stranger from outside, however, given that Alf says he was in his box at the entrance during that period.'

'I don't know about that,' said Freddy. 'I've noticed Alf isn't exactly conscientious about staying at his post, although he denies it. I should have thought it wouldn't have been too difficult for somebody to creep in without his noticing. However, one certainly couldn't count on getting past him safely, and as you say it's far more likely that it was someone Dinah knew at the theatre. By the way, she had a young man until recently, who didn't take it especially well when she ended things. You might want to find out where he was during the vital period. He worked here with the builders for a while, so knew the lay-out of the place.' He frowned as he spoke.

'What is it?' said Entwistle.

'It's funny, but I can't help thinking the building works have something to do with all this.'

'Why should they?'

'I don't know, but I have the strangest feeling that none of this would have happened if Septimus Gooch hadn't fallen out with his builder and forced everyone to cram together in this corridor.'

'I can't see a logical connection myself.'

'Nor can I. Perhaps I'm imagining things.'

Entwistle regarded him directly.

'You've been talking to these people recently. What do you think has been going on?'

'I don't know,' answered Freddy honestly. 'It seems almost impossible to believe that there could be three deaths in one theatre in the space of two months without their being connected in some way. And yet I can't see how at present. As far as I know nobody had a reason to kill either Dinah Belmonte or Una Bryant, and everybody had a motive to kill Septimus Gooch. If I were going to jump to unwarranted conclusions I'd guess that Septimus's death was the main object of all this, that Dinah was killed because she knew who killed him and had to be silenced for it, and that Una's death was either incidental or coincidental. Could Spooner have killed Septimus, by the way? He was wandering around the Jollity at the right time, as at least two of the girls saw him in the back corridor that night.'

'Yes, we thought of that, but nobody else admits to having seen him that evening, and Spooner himself denies leaving the props room during the show. He says the only reason he was in the Jollity at all that evening was because his leg was giving him gyp, and he usually stayed well clear of the theatre as long as anybody else was in it. However, he certainly had a grudge against Gooch. Of course, there's still no evidence that Gooch was killed deliberately.'

'No, but I've a feeling in my bones that he was,' said Freddy. 'All these happenings can't be coincidence, surely?'

'It does seem odd,' Entwistle agreed. 'Well, I'll put Bird onto looking at the post-mortem reports for Una Bryant and Gooch. Perhaps there was something the chaps missed when they did the examination.'

'I've been wondering whether they mightn't have been poisoned,' ventured Freddy. 'They were both found without a mark on them, unless you count the whack on the head Septimus got when he fell backwards. One wouldn't have expected that for Septimus in particular if he'd been felled by a well-placed sock on the jaw, which would surely have left a bruise. Would the doctor who carried out the autopsy have looked for poison?'

'I imagine so, especially if there was no obvious cause of death.'

'Well, other than that I have no suggestions to give, unless there really is a homicidal ghost rampaging around the theatre, striking down people all over the place.'

Freddy took his leave, promising to telephone if anything new occurred to him, and went back to the *Clarion*'s offices, where instead of getting back to work he took a pencil and wrote everything down he could think of that related to the mysterious events at the Jollity Theatre. He wrote down everybody's name and drew a circle around each and lines connecting them, criss-crossing the page. He scrawled notes underneath each name and queries in the margin, ending in many large, ornate question-marks. Then he sat back and stared at the paper. Nothing was any clearer.

One thing he had got wrong in his conversation with Inspector Entwistle was to say that Una's death had been incidental. He remembered now that it could not have been so because Dinah had known something about it, and he was certain that was the reason she had been killed. Dinah had been worried about the ghost, but she had also known or guessed something about how *Una* died, not Septimus. That implied Una had been killed deliberately, because otherwise why should anyone have wanted to kill Dinah? Perhaps Spooner really was the murderer, then. He had been living clandestinely in the theatre since at least the time of Una's death, for she had seen him on the night she died. Had Spooner also killed Septimus? He certainly had a motive for that. Yes, that would make sense. If Bert Spooner had killed Septimus because Septimus would not let Jinks out of his contract, and then murdered Una to keep her quiet—no, that did not work, for Una had died long before Septimus. Well, then, had Spooner killed Una first for some reason, and then killed Septimus to keep him quiet because he knew something about Una's death?

It was all quite baffling. Freddy threw down his pencil impatiently and decided to think about something else. He telephoned Gertie at her family's hunting-lodge in Norfolk, but was informed that her young ladyship was out, so he returned to brooding over the case, to no avail. The whole thing was like a tangled ball of wool: whenever he pulled at one end it fastened itself up all the tighter. Perhaps there was no solving it.

Chapter Sixteen

THE MATTER of Dinah Belmonte's death was of course not only reported in London, but very quickly travelled the length of the country and found its way into the provincial press too. 'Chorus Girl Found Dead In Trunk' was the breathless headline in a hundred local papers that were more accustomed to printing stories about charitable sales of work and cows trapped in ditches than about events many miles away in a remote city. The story was mentioned everywhere from the serious newspapers to the pictorial publications, and the faces of Dinah and the rest of the cast of *Have At It!* were soon familiar at breakfast-tables the length and breadth of Britain, to the accompaniment of much shaking of the head and moralizing at the wickedness that was to be found in the capital and the theatre world in general.

Each member of the company at the Jollity reacted to the horrifying events of the weekend in different ways. Loveday Curtis affected to be desperately upset, but was in reality doing her best to make the most of the attention, while the same was true of Rupert St. Clair to a lesser extent. Morry Jinks was decidedly resentful at the prospect of losing his partner to a

possible murder charge, while Desirée looked openly frightened and Trenton agonized over how to cheer her up. The
chorus as a whole were in a nervous and highly-strung state,
and Jenny was forced to use all her powers of soothing to calm
them down. Alf, meanwhile, was having to be permanently on
guard to keep curious members of the public out of the
theatre, and the extra work did little for his temper.

A second consequence of the story's getting out was that
ticket sales for *Have At It!* increased markedly, and the
company began playing to a packed house, much to Jenny
Minter's surprise and half-guilty gratification, for she felt one
ought not to benefit from a young girl's untimely death. Still,
even though she was sincerely upset at what had happened,
she was enough of a business-woman not to look a gift horse
in the mouth, and therefore let it be known discreetly that she
had no objection to any member of the cast's speaking to the
press about it if they liked, for she knew the value of free
publicity.

On Wednesday evening Freddy went to the Jollity after the
performance and found Jenny looking through a sheaf of
papers in her dressing-room.

'Things are a little trying at present,' she said in answer to
his inquiry. 'Of course we have to have the police here
because of poor Dinah, but they have been getting in the way,
rather.'

'They're certainly drawing a crowd,' observed Freddy.
'There were half a dozen people gawping outside when I
came in.'

'Oh yes! I know I oughtn't to be pleased about the attention, and how the ticket sales are going, but really one couldn't
ask for better advertising, especially just before we go on tour.
I feel almost grubby taking advantage of it, but business is
business, after all.'

She threw the papers to one side and as she did so a note

fluttered to the floor. Freddy hastened to pick it up for her. She glanced at it.

'What's this? Where did this come from? *"Jenny. Must speak to you urgently about Septimus. Will call you tomorrow. Max."* It's dated the 25th of October. Oh dear, that's weeks ago. Did he come in and leave it when I wasn't here? Why didn't I see it?'

'Perhaps you put something on top of it,' suggested Freddy.

'I expect that's it. I'm rather untidy, I'm afraid. Well, never mind—I've spoken to him several times since then. He probably wanted to speak to me about the money he owed Septimus.'

Freddy pricked up his ears.

'Oh?'

'Yes. Poor Max—he's quite hopeless with money and was forever having to borrow it to put on his productions. Of course, that's all very well when they're selling out, but there were a couple of plays recently that folded soon after they opened. Septimus had lent him some money and was bothering Max for repayment. But I'm rather more lenient about things and I've given him an extension.'

'25th of October—that's the day Septimus died. Did Max leave the note that same evening?'

'I don't know. It might not have been the evening—perhaps it was during the matinée.'

'You didn't see him at all?'

'No. I suppose he must have popped in and out when we were all onstage.'

Someone came in wanting to talk to her just then, so Freddy was forced to leave it at that. He retreated into the corridor and saw Peggy just coming out of her dressing-room in her coat and hat, ready to go home.

'Peggy,' he said, 'do you remember telling me that one of the girls saw Max D'Auberville coming out of Jenny's dressing-room a few weeks ago? I can't remember who it was.'

'It was Joyce, I think.'

'Was it the night Septimus died?'

'I couldn't tell you. But she's still here, so why don't you ask her?'

She went back into the dressing-room and re-emerged shortly afterwards in company with the girl in question.

'Yes it was, now you come to mention it,' said Joyce in reply to Freddy's query. 'It was during the second act. I remember because the fastening on my pirate hat had come undone and I had to dash back to the dressing-room between *Blowing Up a Storm* and the cannibal scene to pin it so it wouldn't come off when I did my flip-flops across the stage. I was dashing back to the wings again when I just glimpsed him coming out of Jenny's room. I know it was the same night because I remember thinking afterwards that for all I knew Mr. Gooch might have been lying there already dead in Loveday's room while I was pinning my hat, and I wouldn't have known it.'

'What time was it when you saw him?'

'Er...' she said doubtfully, looking at Peggy, who said:

'The cannibal scene starts at twenty to ten or thereabouts, so it must have been a couple of minutes before that.'

'And where did he go after that?'

'I couldn't tell you. I didn't stop to chat, as I only had a few seconds to get back onstage.'

'And you're sure it was Max D'Auberville you saw?'

'Well, I couldn't swear to it, but I thought it was. He was the right height.'

'Why didn't you mention this at the time?' asked Freddy.

'Because nobody asked me,' replied Joyce, as though it were obvious.

Peggy had begun to understand.

'Do you think Max might have killed old Gooch?' she said in a low voice once Joyce had gone.

'It's a thought,' replied Freddy.

'But then what about Dinah? Was that Max too?'

Freddy did not know. All he knew was that here was a new knot in the already tangled skein of questions that needed answering, and the only way to find out what Max D'Auberville had been doing at the Jollity Theatre that night —if he had indeed been there—was to ask him.

Fortunately, an opportunity presented itself very shortly. The next morning he arrived at the office to find Lady Featherstone drifting vaguely around the news-room. Mr. Bickerstaffe was following her round, wearing an ingratiating smile that looked as though it hurt his face.

'Hallo, Lady F,' said Freddy. 'Glorious weather for the time of year, what?'

'Good morning, Freddy,' she replied. 'I was hoping to see you. I wanted to make sure you have quite recovered from your little accident with the bullseye.'

'My little what? Oh yes,' he said hurriedly as he remembered. 'No permanent harm done, thank you—just a frog in the throat for a few days that's wholly cleared up now.'

'I don't blame you for being overcome by the experience. Have you seen the marvellous reviews for *Consider the Ravens*? For myself I haven't seen such an affecting piece in years. Max D'Auberville is tremendously talented. Sir Aldridge and I were introduced to him a few days ago and found him delightful. I told him how much we had enjoyed the play, and he seemed genuinely pleased, and not at all puffed up. As one of the founding members of the London Ladies' Thespian Association I told him I am determined to take an interest in him. I believe the arts are of the utmost importance. You must write a piece on him, mustn't he, Mr. Bickerstaffe? I'm sure he'd be delighted to speak to you.'

'That's an idea,' said Freddy. 'I shall have to get his number. It's only a pity I didn't think to introduce myself to him after the performance that night.'

'I don't know that you could have, as he didn't stay for the whole play.' She lowered her voice confidentially. 'As a matter of fact, I'm rather pleased about that, as he was sitting in the seat in front of me, and he's such a *tall* man I could hardly see a thing. Fortunately, at a certain point he left his seat and didn't come back. I imagine he went backstage to speak to the actors.'

So Lady Featherstone could bear witness that Max D'Auberville had absented himself from his seat! This was a stroke of good luck that Freddy had not expected.

'What time did he go?' he asked.

She did not seem to think it an odd question.

'Let me see. It was quite a way into the second act—yes, I remember particularly because I was terribly relieved afterwards not to have missed the scene in which the child has its eyes pecked out by the wild birds—such a significant moment and so relevant to the meaning of the whole. I believe it might have been half past nine or so.'

That tallied with what Joyce had said. If Max had left his seat at the Calliope at half past nine, it would have taken him only a minute or two to walk down the alley and in through the stage door of the Jollity. Freddy thought he remembered Trenton saying that Septimus did not usually come to the theatre on a Saturday. Suppose Max had known that, and had gone to speak to Jenny to ask her to intercede on his behalf in the matter of the loan. Suppose he had scribbled her the note and come out of her room, and had then bumped into Septimus unexpectedly. What might have happened next? Freddy could easily see a situation in which Max had decided to take the bull by the horns and speak to Septimus about the money in person. Perhaps their conversation had degenerated into a row, and Max had lashed out in frustration, catching Septimus unawares and causing him to topple over and catch his head on the corner of the cabinet. If anyone could have laid Septimus out it was Max, who was tall and well-built, and now here was definite evidence placing him in the Jollity at that time.

Freddy was becoming more and more excited by his idea. Here at last was a possible handle on the death of Septimus Gooch, which had seemed so inexplicable until now. If his theory was correct it had not been murder exactly, but the unfortunate outcome of a physical fight. Had it taken place in a larger room or outside, then Septimus would have been knocked backwards but would most likely not have come to much harm. As it was, the cramped space, full of furniture with hard corners, had proved fatal.

It was not a perfect theory, however, for there were some questions that remained unanswered. Why had nobody heard the row? The performance was loud, but surely Alf or even Joyce would have heard something if Max and Septimus had become caught up in an altercation during those few minutes —especially since, according to Joyce's story, Max had been wandering around the theatre *in between* musical numbers, when the noise level would have been lower. Then there was the baffling lack of marks on Septimus's body other than the wound on his head. And what of Una and Dinah? Where did they come in? Did they come in at all, in fact? Had there perhaps been two separate crimes? Had Dinah been murdered for a completely different reason, perhaps because of what she knew about Una's death? It seemed the most incredible coincidence, but Freddy had heard of stranger things in his time at the *Clarion*, and although unlikely it was certainly not impossible. He decided to forget the girls for the present and concentrate first on proving that Max had killed Septimus.

The first thing to do was to speak to Max D'Auberville and get his version of events. Strictly speaking Freddy knew it ought to be left to the police, and so he reluctantly telephoned Inspector Entwistle, fully intending to invite himself along to the interview with Max. The inspector was out, however.

Freddy sat at his desk and drummed his fingers for several minutes, but eventually could stand it no longer. He decided to go and speak to Max himself.

After one or two telephone-calls, he eventually ran D'Auberville to ground in the wings of the Calliope Theatre, where he was engaged in speaking to a stage-hand about some urgent matter of scenery. As Freddy waited, to his surprise Loveday Curtis came out of a room close by, looking at her most bewitching and expensive.

'I must go, Max,' she called. 'You won't forget, will you? Oh, it's you,' she said, upon seeing Freddy.

'I didn't know you were acquainted with Max D'Auberville,' he said.

'Yes, we're old friends,' she replied.

'Isn't it early for you to be out and about? I thought theatre people slept late.'

'I have an appointment with the Calvert's Cold Cream people, so I decided to drop in on Max on the way.'

'Calvert's Cold Cream?'

'I let them use my name and a photograph in their advertisements,' she explained.

'Does it pay well?'

'Well enough. But I shall be having a word with them this afternoon, and if I'm not much mistaken it's about to pay even better,' she said complacently. 'I'm becoming rather widely known these days, you see.'

'Ah yes—Dinah. Murder does tend to bring a lot of attention from the press.'

The satisfied smile disappeared immediately and she glared at him.

'It's nothing to do with Dinah. Of course I've been devastated by the whole thing, but this is quite a separate matter. One can't spend forever moping in one's room. Life must go on.'

She tossed her head and stalked off haughtily.

Max D'Auberville had by now finished instructing the stage-hand and Freddy went to introduce himself.

'A friend of Lady Featherstone's, eh?' said Max. 'Delightful woman, and a most generous patron of the arts.'

Freddy had expected it would take some ingenuity to bring the conversation around to what he really wanted to talk about, but as it turned out Max was quite happy to discuss anything Freddy cared to mention. He had no hesitation in admitting that he had owed Septimus money.

'Cerebral plays such as *Ravens* can have a little trouble attracting investment,' he said, waving a hand expansively. 'The man in the street tends to pass them by, preferring the lighter sort of entertainment, and so it can be difficult to raise the money to stage a piece like this one. But Septimus understood the value of strong meat over spun sugar, and was only too happy to extend funds for as long as I needed them. "Max," he said, "if *Ravens* doesn't run for two years solid and then go on to a sell-out tour of the provinces, I'll eat my hat." He was practically begging me to take his money. And he was right, too—why, look how well we're doing! The critics are quite raving about it.'

'I could rave about it myself,' replied Freddy truthfully. 'It's interesting what you say, though. I thought I'd heard that Septimus was tired of waiting for his money and was demanding you pay him back immediately. I expect I must have got hold of the wrong end of the stick.'

'Who said that?' said Max sharply. 'It couldn't be further from the truth. *Ravens* is as safe as houses, and if anybody has been implying it isn't I should like a word with him. If that sort of rumour gets out it can cause trouble.'

'I beg your pardon, it was obviously a mistake. Even so, it's a pity about Septimus's sudden death, isn't it? I suppose that will complicate matters for you financially.'

'Not in the least. Jenny's a good friend of mine, and she's promised to give me as much time as I need to pay back the funds,' replied Max, apparently forgetting what he had just said. 'In fact, we've been talking about her backing another little venture of mine, but it's early days yet.'

'The inquest said it was accidental death, although they couldn't say what led to it exactly. You knew him well—what do you think? You saw him on the night he died, didn't you?'

'Did I? I don't believe so.'

'You were certainly at the Jollity that evening. Jenny found a note you'd left, asking to speak to her urgently. It was dated the day he died.'

Max waved a hand.

'Oh, I'm dreadful with dates. I get them wrong all the time. I shouldn't take any date written by me as gospel.'

'And one of the girls from the chorus saw you there on the same night.'

'Did she, now?' said Max, eyeing Freddy. He did not seem especially pleased to have had the fact brought to his attention. 'Well, then, yes I did leave Jenny a note, but I had no idea it was on the evening that Septimus died. What an extraordinary coincidence!'

'You're quite sure you didn't see Septimus while you were there? I'm sorry to press you, it's just the police are sniffing round now and I've been asked to help them in their inquiries.'

This was stretching the truth slightly, but Max was unsuspicious.

'The police?' he said in alarm. 'Whatever for?'

'Because of the death of Dinah Belmonte.'

Max seemed relieved.

'Oh, I see, the girl in the trunk. What has that to do with Septimus?'

'They think there might be a connection.'

'Really? Goodness me! No, I didn't see anyone. I came in, left Jenny a note and went out again. I didn't see Septimus at all.'

So far, so good. Assuming Max was lying, there was nothing here to disprove Freddy's theory. But what about Dinah?

'I don't suppose you came into the Jollity last Saturday, did you?' he asked.

'Certainly not. I was dining with friends that night and never went near the place.'

'Mind telling me what time you got home?'

You're very curious,' said Max. 'If you must know, we watched the performance of *Ravens*, then afterwards went to Babcock's and I arrived home shortly after one o'clock.'

And that was all Freddy could get out of him. He was not of the police and could not insist on Max's furnishing him with an alibi, but at least he had some useful information for Inspector Entwistle. The plain fact was that Max D'Auberville had had ample opportunity to kill Septimus Gooch. Further-more, he had attended a performance of his own play on the night of Dinah's death, and had therefore been in the vicinity of the Jollity Theatre at the vital time. The thing to do now was to find out whether Max had had any opportunity to steal into the Jollity and kill Dinah without being seen, and after that begin looking into his whereabouts on the night Una had died.

'Kind of you to look me up,' said Max. 'You must come and see *Ravens* again. I shall give you free tickets.' He held up a hand before Freddy could object. 'No, I won't hear a word of argument—it's the least I can do for a friend of Lady Feather-stone's. She's done so much for the theatre, and your paper has printed some highly flattering things about the production —thanks to you, no doubt. Think of it as a token of my appreciation.'

Freddy, who was firmly resolved never to sit through *Consider the Ravens* ever again, thanked him and took his leave.

Chapter Seventeen

Freddy had not got very far down the street when he heard footsteps behind him and a voice saying, 'Excuse me, sir.' He turned to see a young man of the working type who was in his shirt sleeves and had evidently followed him out of the theatre.

'Yes?' he said.

'I beg your pardon, I heard you talking to Mr. D'Auberville and thought I heard you say you'd come from the Jollity Theatre and were working for the police.'

'More or less,' said Freddy. 'What is it?'

The young man shuffled hesitantly.

'My name's Payne—Cyril Payne. Dinah Belmonte was a friend of mine.'

'I see. I'm sorry.'

'It's terrible what happened to her, sir. I've not slept a wink since I heard it.'

'You were fond of her, I take it?'

'She's the reason I started working at the theatre here.' He gestured back towards the Calliope. 'I was working for Wilkerson's—that's the building firm—until a couple of months ago. We did a job at the Jollity, and that's where I met her.'

Freddy looked at Cyril with sudden interest. This, presumably, was Dinah's young man, who had said something that had made her think, and had perhaps set in motion the train of events that had led to her death.

'We got friendly for a while and I don't mind admitting I liked her,' Cyril went on. 'But I suppose she was too good for the likes of me. She was pretty and could sing and dance, and she rubbed shoulders with famous actors and actresses, and she was going to be a star one day. I'm just a plain working man and proud of my trade.'

'What is your trade?'

'I'm a carpenter, sir, but I can turn my hand to most jobs —plastering, plumbing, electrical work—that sort of thing. I worked at the Jollity for a month or two, and as I say Dinah and I were friendly for a while until she ended it. I don't want you to think there were any hard feelings on my side,' he added quickly. 'I don't mind saying I was upset at first, and I'd have liked to keep seeing her, but you can't force a girl to like you, can you? So I did my best to accept it.'

'Did she get you the job at the Calliope?'

'Not exactly. But she put the theatre into my mind and it wouldn't leave. While we were walking out and I was seeing all these theatre-folk every day I got bitten by the bug, as they say, and somehow I couldn't keep away. I just liked the smell of it and the excitement, and once I'd been at the Jollity a few weeks I knew I couldn't stay in my old job. Besides, I wasn't happy with the way old Wilkerson worked. He took on cheap labour and cut corners and bodged things together. So I took what was owed me and came for the job here. It's only till the end of the run but if I do well they say they'll put in a word for me with one of the companies that do the big theatre productions, so I can keep doing this sort of work.'

'You prefer building scenery to all the other stuff, eh?'

'I do. If it goes well I've a mind to set up my own firm one day.' He swallowed. 'But I've not been able to buckle down to my work since I heard about Dinah. It's terrible what the papers are saying—that she was strangled and hidden in a trunk. Is that true?'

'I'm afraid it is. By the way, I rather think the police would like to speak to you about that.'

Cyril stared at him in surprise.

'To me? Why? They don't think I did it, do they?'

'They're certainly keen to eliminate you from their inquiries. When young ladies are murdered the police tend to look suspiciously at chaps they'd been friendly with, you see.'

Cyril flushed.

'I'd never have laid a finger on her, and you can tell the police that!' he said heatedly. 'They're welcome to come and talk to me if they like. I'm an honest man and I've nothing to hide.'

'I'm pleased to hear it. Then I dare say you won't mind telling me whether you went anywhere near the Jollity on Saturday evening.'

'No, I didn't. I was at a musical evening in Bethnal Green on Saturday evening until late.'

'Are there witnesses to prove it?'

'I should say so—about a hundred.'

'What time did it finish?'

'Late—a quarter past eleven, I think it was.'

'And where did you go after that?'

'Why, I went straight home.'

'Did anyone see you?'

'Yes—I lodge with a married couple who like that sort of thing, and we all went to the meeting together and then came home. They'll tell you.'

'Lucky for you if that's true.'

'It is, I swear it, and if you'll tell me who to ask for, I'll go and speak to the police straightaway and clear my name.'

'That's the spirit! Once they've scratched you off the list

they'll be able to concentrate on finding the chap who really did it.'

Cyril clenched his fists indignantly.

'I hope they do get him. It's not right, what was done to her. I should like to see whoever did it hang.'

'In that case, perhaps you might be able to help me. You see, the police can't find a motive for Dinah's murder, and I've been wondering whether she was killed because she knew something.'

'About what?'

'It's a long story, but there have been two other deaths at the Jollity recently, and no-one seems to be sure whether they were killed deliberately—or even how they died. The first was a girl called Una Bryant, who danced with Dinah in the chorus and was found dead in her dressing-room. It was thought to be the work of a ghost—yes, you may well look disbelieving, and rightly so, because it's all been proved to be nonsense. Still, when I was talking to Dinah she gave me the distinct impression that she knew or had an idea of what had happened to Una. But she didn't tell me exactly what it was, only that she'd got the idea from you.'

'From me? What did I say?'

'That's just it—she didn't tell me. All she said was that it was something you'd said and that it had made her wonder.'

Cyril looked blank.

'Well, I don't know what it might be, sir. We talked about lots of things. She told me theatre stories and I told her about the goings-on at my firm—although my stories weren't as interesting as hers. I'm afraid I mainly complained about Mr. Wilkerson and how he didn't do things as he ought.'

'Did she mention Max D'Auberville at all? Did she know him?'

'Not as far as I know—leastways, only as far as everyone in the theatre knows everyone else. She never talked about him in particular. You don't think he had anything to do with it, do you?'

'I don't know. He seems to spend a lot of time at the Jollity, that's all.'

'It's just next door,' said Cyril reasonably. 'But why would he want to go killing anybody?'

'I wish I knew.'

Cyril seemed to be thinking. At last he shook his head.

'I'm sure I don't know what Dinah was talking about. I don't remember saying anything that might have put her in danger. What could I have said? I don't know anything about what's been going on at the Jollity.'

Freddy handed him a card.

'Well, if anything does spring to mind you'll let me know, won't you?'

'I will. I'll do anything I can to help you find the—the—I won't say the word I'm thinking of—I'll just call him the rotter who did it,' replied Cyril. He made to leave, then turned back and gave a little huff of amusement. 'Ghosts, eh? They're a superstitious lot, theatre people, aren't they?'

'Yes, well as it turns out Una herself was one of the ghosts. It seems sound carries down one of the pipes in the new cloak-room to a dressing-room on the other corridor, and she and some of the other girls including Dinah were going in there and whispering down it as a sort of practical joke.'

'Chorus-girls are a caution and no mistake,' said Cyril, with the wisdom of three months' experience. 'Well, I'll let you know if I remember what it is I'm supposed to have said. I won't let this murderer get off scot-free if I can help it.'

'Nor will I,' said Freddy.

Chapter Eighteen

AFTER HIS CONVERSATION with Cyril Payne, Freddy went to
Scotland Yard to report to Inspector Entwistle the result of his
interview with Max D'Auberville. The inspector was not especially pleased that Freddy had acted without consulting him
first, but he was forced to admit that Max's presence in the
Jollity Theatre at the time of Septimus Gooch's death looked
suspicious, and that it might be worth investigating his movements further.

'I thought this was a simple enough case,' he said. 'You
wouldn't think it would be difficult to find out who killed one
girl in a theatre where everyone is wandering about and a
murderer would be easy to spot. But it seems everybody was
too busy rushing to get out of the place and off to parties and
suchlike.'

'And the back corridor wasn't very much in use, so if she
went up there it's quite feasible that nobody would see what
happened,' Freddy observed.

'We'll have to take a close look at the alibi of this Payne
chap. Spurned young men are always a fair bet when it comes
to dead girls.'

'I hope he wasn't our murderer as I rather liked him,' said

Freddy. 'He struck me as a particularly upright fellow, and he claims to have been attending an evening of wholesome musical entertainment during the vital period.'

'We'll see about that,' replied Entwistle darkly. He wrinkled his brow in annoyance. 'I don't like this case. There are too many dead people and not enough reasons for it.'

'There were plenty of reasons to kill Septimus, if it was deliberate. Did you learn anything from the post-mortem report, by the way?'

'Not much. There were no bruises or signs of a fight— although I didn't expect there would be, as it would have been mentioned at the inquest.'

'There must be lots of ways of laying a man out other than hitting him,' said Freddy thoughtfully.

'Such as?'

'Oh, I don't know—a rug on a slippery floor, perhaps.'

'The room was fully carpeted,' Entwistle pointed out.

'Yes, it was, wasn't it? Well, then, perhaps a trip-wire across the room, fastened close to the carpet so it wouldn't easily be seen. Have you looked for something of the kind?'

'I wasn't on duty that night, but I expect all possibilities were considered at the time. Besides, I can think of two reasons why a trip-wire's not the answer: one, the room was occupied by Loveday Curtis, who would surely have tripped over the thing herself; and two, a trip-wire implies some kind of premeditation, which lets out Max D'Auberville, who wouldn't have had the time or opportunity to rig up such a thing.'

'True,' said Freddy. 'But I won't be defeated. There must be something we're missing. You can't deny that Max is a good candidate for a murderer.'

'Well, we'll see what we can dig up about him, and whether there's a connection between him and Dinah Belmonte. It's certainly worth looking into.'

He waved a hand to indicate that his visitor was dismissed.

Freddy took the hint and left. He glanced at his watch. It was a matinée afternoon at the Jollity, and all the cast would be there by now. He decided to go and see if there had been any further developments. Alf admitted him grudgingly and he went to knock on Jenny's door to let her know of his presence. Nobody answered, so he went to Trenton's room, where Trenton and Jinks were readying themselves for the performance.

'Hallo, Freddy,' Trenton said glumly. 'Any news from the police? Are we all about to be arrested?'

'I don't think so.'

'I'm certain it must have been someone from outside. After all, which of us would want to kill Dinah? Quite apart from anything else, it leaves us a girl short.'

'Spoken like a true show-man,' said Freddy.

Trenton went on:

'This whole thing has put the wind up us all, I don't mind saying. Who would have thought such a thing could happen in our little company?'

Freddy was about to ask a question when there came the sound of a commotion out in the corridor. A man's raised voice could be heard, followed by a gasp from Desirée as Alf said roughly: 'You can't come in here. Get out!'

Freddy and Trenton went out to find out what was happening, and saw that a man sporting battered old tweeds and a glorious moustache had come in through the stage door and was attempting to get past Alf, who was refusing to give way, causing the stranger to go red with irritation.

'Let me past!' he snapped, trying to step round Alf, who moved to block his way.

'Not so fast. This is private property and I'm not about to let the likes of you in however much you shout. Who d'you think you are, anyway?'

The man drew himself up.

'Who am I, sir? Who am I? I am Lord Oakford, and this young lady is my daughter, who has no business in this place.'

'Father!' said Desirée, who had gone pale under her grease-paint. 'I didn't expect to see you here!'

'No, I don't suppose you did,' he replied stiffly. 'It is quite clear your intention has been to conceal yourself as thoroughly as possible since you took it into your head to run away. Not a letter or a telephone-call have we had for nearly six months. We have scoured London for you, placed advertisements, and had the police searching for you, all to no avail —until this morning, when I opened my newspaper to find your photograph staring back at me, and discovered you have spent all this time cavorting with a pack of *mummers*. I dare say your mother will never get over the shock. She was prostrate in her room when I left her.'

Staring at Desirée, Freddy was suddenly visited by a flash of memory.

'I knew I'd seen your face somewhere before!' he exclaimed. 'Of course—you're Deborah Allbright, the missing heiress who ran away from her wedding to Viscount Kimmerston back in the spring.'

'Good God!' said Trenton, flabbergasted. 'Is it true, Desirée?'

'Yes,' she replied faintly.

'It was quite a story earlier this year,' Freddy went on. 'As I recall the *Clarion* was offering a reward of five pounds to the person who found you. Nobody claimed it, and yet you've been here all this time, singing and dancing in full view of eight hundred people for ten performances a week.' He began to laugh. 'I say, you must have a nerve of iron.'

'I haven't, really,' she said. 'I did it because I couldn't help it. It's got into my blood now, and I must be on the stage or I believe I'd die. I wanted to do it years ago but Father and Mother wouldn't hear of it, so I thought that was that and resolved to try and forget about it if I could. Then Gerald asked me to marry him and I said yes—I don't know why, I must have been mad—and the wedding-day came closer and closer, and I didn't know how to get out of it because Mother had invited half the county and Gerald's people were going to move out of the Old Hall and give it to him. But the idea of being stuck in a draughty old pile in the wilds of Northumberland with nothing to look at except trees and nobody to talk to except Gerald made me realize I should go out of my mind with boredom if I went through with the thing. So I made a bolt for it and came down to London.

'I was going to stay at a hotel for a few days and then telephone to explain what I'd done. But then I thought about all the people I'd let down, and about how the guests would be gossiping about it, and about what I'd say to Gerald—I mean, what *can* one say? "I'm sorry, Gerald, I never loved you and I only agreed to marry you because Mother suggested it and I couldn't think of a good reason to say no." So I put off the call and went wandering around London for a bit to get things straight in my head. Then I saw they were holding auditions for a part in *Have At It!* and I thought it couldn't do any harm to try for it, just for fun. I made up a name and told them I'd lived in Canada and invented a theatre company there I'd supposedly performed with, and to my surprise they didn't ask for references but let me sing. And I got the part!' She flushed and her eyes were bright at the remembrance. 'I didn't know a thing about performing, but somehow I got by, and after the first week I knew the theatre was where I was meant to be and I could never go home again. I'm sorry, Father,' she faltered. 'I wanted to call, I really did, but I knew if I did you'd make me come away, and I couldn't face that.'

'Weren't you frightened you'd be found out?' asked Freddy.

'A little. But nobody here seemed to care about my past as long as I could play my part well, and I suppose I managed that all right. As for everybody else—well, we didn't do the London season so I knew nobody of my own sort was likely to recognize me. I thought the fuss in the newspapers would die down sooner or later, but I dyed my hair and had it cut in a different style just to be on the safe side, so I was fairly sure I wouldn't be spotted. I did have one narrow escape a few weeks ago, when I nearly ran into Gerald in Hyde Park.' She turned to Trenton. 'I was with you that day, and I had to make a run for it. I don't expect you remember.'

'I vaguely recall something of the kind,' replied Trenton with a belated attempt at insouciance.

Lord Oakford had been listening to all this with an air of surprise and displeasure.

'This is all very well,' he growled. 'But the fact remains I do not want to see my daughter on the stage. Ours is an old and respected family, and we can't have that sort of thing going on. Who is in charge here?'

'I am,' replied Jenny, who had just arrived. 'What seems to be the problem?'

There was some confusion as everyone attempted to explain the situation to her at once. At last she understood.

'Goodness, I had no idea of this!' She regarded Desirée a moment, her head on one side, then laughed. 'I expect I ought to sack you for applying to us under false pretences, but really, you've done such a wonderful job I can't see anyone else in the rôle at present.' She turned to Lord Oakford. 'You have a very talented daughter, Lord Oakford. I don't suppose you read the trade papers, but the critics have said some very flattering things about her performance.'

This was not what Lord Oakford wanted to hear.

'Never mind that. I won't stand for any daughter of mine flaunting herself for public display. Deborah, I told you years ago to forget all this nonsense, although I expect I ought to have known to search the theatres given this craze of yours for acting. Still, one might have hoped you would have chosen

Shakespeare rather than this low sort of entertainment. Now, you'll come with me at once, do you hear?'

Desirée gaped at him in horror.

'But I can't!'

'She can't go now, she's needed for the show!' exclaimed Jenny in dismay. 'The curtain goes up in less than half an hour.'

'Madam, until my daughter is of age, I am the one who will decide whether she is needed or not, and by whom. I think you will find the law is on my side.'

'Father——' began Desirée. She threw a pleading look at Trenton, who for the first time in his life saw a chance to act the hero, and took it. He stepped forward and held out a hand to Lord Oakford.

'Trenton Bagshawe, sir. My father was the Bishop of Tewkesbury. I believe you were at Oxford with him.'

Lord Oakford frowned.

'Bagshawe...Bagshawe. You don't mean old Forbes Bagshawe? Why yes, I remember him. So you're his son, are you? And on the stage too? Good Lord—does this pass as fashion among the young people of today?'

'No sir, I just like singing to an audience,' replied Trenton simply. 'But look here, I wanted to say that you needn't worry one bit about Desirée—I beg your pardon, Deborah. I've been keeping an eye on her and she's been perfectly safe here. I promise you if I'd seen anything I thought was not quite right I'd have persuaded her to give it up, but everything here is completely above the board.'

Whatever Trenton's faults, there was nothing of the disreputable about him, and he had 'well-bred young gentleman' written quite plainly all over his face. He talked on encouragingly to ease Lord Oakford's evident suspicions that his daughter had fallen into a den of vice and sin.

'You see Miss Minter is in charge of the company, and she's a stickler for proper behaviour, aren't you Jenny?' he said.

She nodded brightly.

'Oh yes.' Having taken the measure of Lord Oakford, she added, 'We gave Lord and Lady Browncliffe a tour of the theatre a few weeks ago and they couldn't find a thing to complain about.'

Talk of the Bishop and the Browncliffes mollified Oakford very slightly, and his moustache ceased to bristle quite so fixedly.

'Why don't you stay and see the show?' suggested Trenton, taking advantage of the pause in hostilities. 'Jenny, could we give Lord Oakford a ticket for a box? I do think we ought to give him a chance to see Deborah properly in her part. Freddy, you'll sit with him, won't you?'

'Certainly,' replied Freddy promptly. The words 'well-bred young gentleman' had perhaps rubbed off at the edges in his case, but he could remember how to play the part when required.

Almost before Oakford knew it he had been accorded the status of guest of honour and furnished with a free ticket to the best seat in the house. He was presented with a printed programme and escorted to the box, and Freddy was given the task of keeping up a stream of entertaining conversation, pointing out the finer architectural details of the theatre and recounting amusing stories of theatrical mishaps until the performance started. He watched his companion carefully during the show, and sensed a softening when Oakford let out a laugh despite himself at Morry Jinks's first comic routine. When Oakford was silent and rapt as Desirée sang her beautiful solo, staring as though he could not believe it, Freddy knew the initial battle had been more or less won. The performers seemed to be putting on a special effort that afternoon, knowing how important it was, and the show was a good one.

'I think he enjoyed it, old chap,' murmured Freddy to Trenton as they returned backstage afterwards. The two of them watched discreetly as Lord Oakford congratulated his daughter stiffly on her performance. It was a touch too rowdy for his taste, he said, but after seeing it he could understand why people liked that sort of thing. After a few minutes he left the theatre and Desirée joined them, a little tearful.

'Everybody has been so kind, although I know I don't deserve it,' she said. 'I don't know how to thank you, Trenton. If it hadn't been for you I'm sure he'd have made a terrible fuss and dragged me out of the theatre, but you calmed him down beautifully.'

'Oh, rather, what?' said Trenton in some confusion.

'But won't he make a fuss another day instead?' asked Freddy. 'He still doesn't seem exactly overjoyed.'

'We're going to go and talk about things now, although I doubt he'll be too pleased when I tell him I'm not coming home. He's dreadfully old-fashioned and doesn't approve of girls earning their own money—especially on the stage, as you can tell—but I shall talk him round one way or another. I'm awfully sorry I didn't say anything before, but I had to keep it a secret, don't you see?'

'Won't you have to speak to—what's his name—Gerald?' Trenton could not help asking.

'Oh, I read in the paper that he married someone else about a month after I left, so I don't think I exactly broke his heart,' she replied.

Before Trenton knew what she was about to do she gave him a kiss on the cheek and left. Trenton's face was a picture.

'I say,' was all he said.

Chapter Nineteen

It was not long until Freddy's detective-work bore fruit, for the following Monday morning he was summoned to Scotland Yard. When he arrived he found Inspector Entwistle in fine good humour.

'I won't deny I had my doubts, but it looks as though you might be on to something,' he said when Freddy arrived.

'Why? What have you got?'

'A disgruntled former stage-manager who fell out with D'Auberville a couple of weeks ago and walked out. People with a grudge aren't usually the most reliable of witnesses, but at least there's no difficulty in getting them to talk.'

'And what did he have to say?'

'He was with Max one day when Septimus came in and started throwing his weight around. It seems Max was much closer to bankruptcy than he was letting on. He was up to the hilt with the banks and they wouldn't lend him another penny, so he went to Septimus and somehow persuaded him to finance *Dry Harvest*, which flopped. He then ran up more debts putting on *Consider the Ravens*, but by this time Septimus was getting impatient and wanted to know when he could expect his money back. Only Max didn't have it, because he's one of these chaps who never has it. This stage-manager was there when Septimus came to the Calliope and threatened Max with the law if he didn't pay the money back by the 27th of October.'

'The 27th? And Septimus died on the 25th. Awfully convenient timing.'

'Awfully, isn't it?' agreed Entwistle. 'Our witness says Max didn't take it well at all.'

'Still, that doesn't necessarily mean he went to the Jollity and whacked old Gooch over the head, does it? What we really need is someone to have seen him going into or coming out of Loveday's room.' Freddy eyed Inspector Entwistle. 'What is it? There's a pleased look about you that suggests you have something else to say. Don't tell me you *have* found someone?'

'As a matter of fact we have.'

'Who?'

'Rupert St. Clair.'

Freddy stared in astonishment.

'Good Lord! St. Clair? What did he say?'

'He says that he was late getting ready for the second act and nearly missed his cue. He doesn't usually go back to his dressing-room during the second half, but he was wondering why he'd been late so went back to the room just quickly to look at his watch, and it turned out it wasn't working.'

'Was this before or after Joyce went to pin her hat?'

'Almost immediately after. As far as I can make out, it happened like this: the chorus had come offstage for a minute or so, waiting to go back on. Joyce ran to her room and when she came out again she saw Max coming out of Jenny Minter's room. She doesn't know where he went after that, but that's where St. Clair takes over, because a few seconds afterwards he also came off the stage and saw Max open Loveday's door. He doesn't think Max saw him. St. Clair then went into his own room and stayed there for a couple of minutes, but says he didn't see anyone on his way back to the stage. That could mean that Max had already left the theatre, or it could mean he was still in Loveday's room murdering Septimus Gooch. Incidentally, I don't know why it should have taken St. Clair more than ten seconds to make sure his watch wasn't working, but that's his story.'

'I expect he didn't go back just to look at his watch.' Freddy made a gesture as of one taking a drink from a glass.

'Oh, it's like that, is it? I see.'

'Have you asked Alf whether he saw any of this?' Freddy wanted to know.

'Alf said he didn't see a thing. Swears he was in his box all the time.'

'Well, that's not true. I saw him wandering around myself that evening. One wonders why they bother with a stage door-keeper. Why, anyone might have come in, tried on all the costumes then burgled the place thoroughly for all Alf would have seen of them. So Max D'Auberville was wandering in and out of all the rooms, including Loveday's, was he? Why didn't Rupert say anything before? Or rather, why has he decided to speak now?'

'It seems Rupert is a little wary of the police for some reason, so when we pressed him politely on one or two matters, he was only too happy to point the finger away from himself. He said it had completely slipped his mind earlier, as there was no question at the time but that Septimus had died by accident, as was subsequently confirmed at the inquest. Whether that's true or not I'll leave it to you to decide. Anyway, once we'd found out that Max had been seen at the Jollity that night we did some more digging and found out one more interesting piece of information. It turns out that Max called his accountant at a quarter past ten and gave him to understand that he wasn't expecting any more trouble from Septimus about the money he owed him.'

'Did he give a reason for that?'

'No, but it's rather suggestive, don't you think? How could he have known there would be no more trouble if he hadn't been aware that the man to whom he was in debt was dead?'

'Well, he did leave a note for Jenny to ask for her help. Perhaps he was feeling confident that she would intercede with Septimus on his behalf.'

Entwistle looked sceptical.

'He must have thought she had a lot of influence to have had that kind of confidence. I think my idea is more likely.'

'I don't suppose you've managed to find out whether Max had the opportunity to kill Dinah, have you?' asked Freddy.

'He might have. It's true that he was with friends on the night in question, as he said, but there was a period shortly after the performance of *Consider the Ravens* ended when he disappeared for a few minutes. He certainly didn't go backstage to speak to his actors, but he might easily have been mingling with the crowd. Nobody saw him at the Jollity that evening, so while he *might* have gone in and done it, we've no proof either way. I wouldn't pin our hopes on that just yet.'

'Have you had the post-mortem examination results for Dinah?'

'Yes—she was strangled all right.'

Freddy's face darkened, remembering Dinah and her fluffy hair and delicate ways.

'I wish I'd asked her what she meant by what she said that day. I can't help thinking she might still be alive if I hadn't let myself get distracted,' he said.

'We may never know,' replied Entwistle. 'But I'd like to get the man who killed her. The question is: was it Max D'Auberville?'

'How do we find out?'

'We politely invite him to come and speak to us.' Entwistle glanced up at a clock on the wall. 'In fact, if I'm not much mistaken, they should be bringing him in very soon.'

Sure enough, shortly afterwards, Max was brought in by

Sergeant Bird and a constable. He was in a highly disgruntled
and unco-operative state and looked slightly dishevelled.

'What time is this to get a man up on a Monday morning?' he demanded.

'Sorry to take you away from your lady friend,' said Bird,
'but the inspector here wants to speak to you. Would you like
to call your solicitor first?'

'What do I need a solicitor for? I've done nothing wrong. I
don't want a solicitor.'

'Very well, then,' said Entwistle. 'We'd like to ask you some
questions about the death of Septimus Gooch.'

'What about it? I don't know anything. It was an accident,
wasn't it?'

'That's what everyone assumed, but we have reason to
believe it may have been murder.'

'Murder? Good God! But why drag me into it?'

'Because you were seen going into Loveday Curtis's dressing-room shortly before Septimus was found dead in that very
room.'

Max's mouth dropped open.

'What? Who—'

'Do you deny you did it?'

'I—' he paused. 'I think perhaps I do need a solicitor after
all.'

Just then there came the sound of a raised female voice
outside the room, and to Freddy's astonishment Loveday
herself burst in.

'Max!' she cried. 'What are they saying?'

'Here,' said Bird. 'I thought we told you to stay where you
were.'

'They think I killed Septimus,' said Max. 'They say
someone saw me going into your dressing-room on the night
he died.'

'What? Did you? You never told me. Did you kill him?
Oh, Max, did you do it for me?' She threw her arms about his

neck. 'I won't let you arrest him. I'll die first!' she announced dramatically. 'Max and I are in love, you see.'

'Are we?' said Max, to whom this seemed to come as a surprise.

'It's true,' she went on. 'He did it for me. He did it for me because Septimus treated me badly.'

'Get away from me,' he said, disentangling her arms from around his neck with difficulty. 'You're quite mad. I never killed anybody.'

'Look, what's all this about?' demanded Entwistle.

'We found this young lady not yet dressed at Mr. D'Auberville's flat when we went there this morning,' replied Sergeant Bird.

'It's early,' said Loveday, primping a little. 'And you took him away before I could gather my thoughts together. But I couldn't possibly leave him alone with the police. I've heard the sort of things you do to break a man's spirit. Don't say anything, Max—not even if they torture you! I'll speak up for you, I promise. I won't let them hang you. You won't get anything out of him, d'you hear?' she said fiercely, turning to Entwistle.

Max turned a pleading eye upon the inspector, who took the hint and said, 'If you'll just wait outside, madam, I'll see to you shortly.'

Loveday was escorted protesting out of the room, a solicitor was summoned, and after some little delay Max told his story. It was true that Septimus had been threatening the law unless Max paid back the money that was owed him. They had been business partners in the past but had parted ways, for Max was all for artistic Truth, while Septimus rated profit over art and believed that the real money was in popular shows. They had remained on cordial terms for some years, and Septimus had financed two or three of Max's productions, but eventually he had tired of throwing his money into a hole in the ground, as he put it, and had started asking for it back. Relations between them gradually deteriorated as it became clear that Max was unlikely ever to be able to repay, and at last Septimus lost his patience and presented Max with an ultimatum: pay back the loan or he would begin legal proceedings. The threat had come at the worst time, for *Consider the Ravens* was Max's most successful production in years, and had Septimus only been prepared to wait a little longer there was every chance he might have recouped at least some of his funds. As it was, his demands threatened to close the production altogether.

It was at this point, while Max was in fear of losing his play, that Loveday had come to him and expressed an interest in becoming a serious actress. She was keen to have a part in one of his future productions, she said. She seemed unhappy, and a little questioning elicited from her that Septimus was treating her cruelly, but she did not know how to end things with him, for she was frightened that if she did Septimus would take it badly and dismiss her from the show. Would Max rescue her from her tormentor? If anyone could stand up to Septimus she knew he could. She spoke most flatteringly of Max and his work, and before he knew it one thing had led to another, and the lady was professing her undying affection for him. Naturally it would have been churlish to spurn her after she had come to him and thrown herself on his mercy, although he was fully aware that Septimus would not take it well if he found out about it, so he swore her to secrecy.

The date for repayment was now fast approaching, and ever the optimist he planned to ask Jenny Minter to intercede with Septimus on his behalf about the loan. With that in mind, on the Saturday night in question, Max had slipped into the Jollity through the stage door just for a minute, intending to speak to Jenny about it. He knew it was safe to do so, for Septimus did not usually come to the theatre on Saturdays. Jenny was onstage so he left a note in her dressing-room, then put his head into Loveday's room just for a second in case she was there. To his enormous astonishment the sight that greeted him was not Loveday, but Septimus Gooch himself, laid out on the floor, stone dead. Assuming he must have been struck down by a heart attack or something of the kind, Max left Septimus where he was and withdrew, for he had an engagement later that evening and did not wish to be held up by doctors and formalities. He readily admitted this was not exactly public-spirited of him, but it was obvious that nothing could be done, so he did not believe he had caused any harm. Septimus would have been just as dead whether Max had called for help or not. He further admitted that his first thought on finding the body was that *Consider the Ravens* was saved, and in his relief he had telephoned his accountant and informed him of that fact.

Other than that he had nothing else to confess. He denied absolutely the charge that Septimus had been very much alive when he went into Loveday's dressing-room, and that he had knocked Septimus over and killed him. He was fond of Loveday, but their entanglement had come about entirely by accident, mainly because he was flattered by her attention and by how much she looked up to him. No, he had not killed Septimus in order to leave the way clear for them to announce their engagement. Why, the very idea was ridiculous. Now, if the police had quite finished he had things to attend to and would like to leave.

The police had not quite finished, as it turned out, for there was another small matter of a dead girl in a trunk to be cleared up. There Max denied absolutely any knowledge of Dinah Belmonte—had never seen her in his life, and had better things to do than go around strangling chorus-girls whenever the whim took him. He reacted with incredulity to the suggestion that he had killed her because she knew or suspected he had murdered Septimus and he was afraid she would give his secret away. No, he had not gone to the Jollity on the night she died, and no, he could not prove it. He had spoken to lots of people in the audience at the Calliope after that evening's performance of *Ravens*, although none that he could name. However, he was sure someone would step forward to exonerate him.

'What do you think of this story of his, then?' Inspector Entwistle inquired of Freddy afterwards. 'Do you think he really did find Septimus already dead?'

'It's possible, I suppose,' replied Freddy. 'But it's a little too convenient for my liking. He had such a beautiful motive to kill him.'

'Yes. I only wish we had more evidence that it *was* murder in Septimus's case, because Max is a perfect candidate for it. I must say I had no idea he was getting up to no good with Loveday Curtis. You wouldn't have thought they were at all well-matched. She's a musical star and he writes heavy allegorical plays, but it sounds as though she pretty much threw herself at him. Why should she do that?'

'I gather Septimus had refused to marry her, and Jenny told me he tended to move easily from one girl to another. I imagine she'd seen the signs and decided to prepare for the worst. From what the girls of the chorus tell me, she's ambitious and ruthless and not above trampling people underfoot on her way to the top. If one man let her down I shouldn't be a bit surprised if she started looking out for another immediately.'

'Well, she may have hitched her wagon to the wrong star this time.'

'Unless it was all deliberate,' suggested Freddy.

'Do you mean Max did it at Loveday's instigation?'

'It would make sense, don't you think? Loveday's completely self-centred and I expect she wouldn't take too kindly to being dropped. I can imagine she might have pestered Max into having it out with Septimus. It might be that he didn't intend to kill him, but that's what happened in the end.'

'Hmm. Well, we can't prove it—and more importantly we've no evidence at all that Max went anywhere near Dinah. That's the real difficulty, of course. She's the only one we can be sure was murdered, so without proof I don't think we'll get very far.'

'That's true. We also don't have any evidence that Dinah knew anything at all about Septimus's death. In fact, I'd rather got the impression it was *Una's* death she was worried about, not Septimus's—and where Una comes in I still have no idea.'

'Well, we'll keep Max here for now, as his little trip into Loveday's dressing-room looks highly suspicious,' said Entwistle. 'And we'll look for his finger-prints on that trunk, just in case. But don't print it in that rag of yours just yet. We've no evidence and we don't want the story being splashed all over London until we're sure we can bring charges against him.'

'I shall be as silent as the grave,' Freddy assured him.

'Are you going back to the Jollity? Keep your ear to the ground, won't you, and let us know if you hear anything— that is, if you can tear your mind away from all those chorus-girls.'

'My mind is eminently above such frivolities,' said Freddy, and went out.

Chapter Twenty

BUT IF FREDDY and the police had hoped to keep Max D'Auberville's arrest quiet, Loveday Curtis had other ideas. When Freddy passed a news-stand on his way to the Jollity at half past five, he found that the *Herald*, rival newspaper of the *Clarion*, had got hold of the story and were giving it full prominence on the front page of their early evening edition. Heart sinking, he bought a copy and read the article, which contained most of the information Inspector Entwistle had asked him to keep quiet—how it had initially been thought that Septimus Gooch had died accidentally, and how the police had changed their mind and come round to the view that it had been murder; Max's visit to Loveday's dressing-room and his claim that he had discovered Septimus already dead; Max's financial dealings with Septimus and his presumed motive for murder; the love triangle between the three of them and Loveday's assertion of cruelty against Septimus—all described in the most lurid manner. Someone had obviously been talking, and from the particular details given in the story it did not take too much intelligence to deduce who it must have been: Loveday Curtis knew an opportunity for publicity when she saw one, and had evidently decided that there was more to be gained than lost from the world's knowing of her connection with Max D'Auberville. A photograph of her at her prettiest accompanied the story, which further announced that charges were expected very soon.

Freddy shoved the newspaper exasperatedly into his pocket and continued on his way to the Jollity, where he found that the news had arrived before him. The chorus in particular were in a state of great merriment at the development, and since Loveday had not arrived yet they were making free with a number of ribald and unflattering remarks, which could be overheard issuing through the open door of their dressing-room. Glancing in as he passed, Freddy saw Maudie applying dark paint from a stick to her eyelids with great concentration, as her sister read the *Herald* with her feet up. They both looked up at once and greeted Freddy cheerfully.

'Have you heard the latest about Loveday and Max?' said Maudie.

Freddy replied in the affirmative.

'She has a cheek!' exclaimed Minnie. 'All that fuss she made about forcing old Goochie to marry her, and all the while she was doing the dirty on him behind his back.'

They seemed much more interested in the affair than in the fact that Max D'Auberville had been arrested.

'Jenny won't want him after that,' said Maudie.

'If you ask me she never wanted him,' replied Minnie. 'He's far too full of himself.' She threw the newspaper aside and looked about for something else to read. Her eye fell on an illustrated magazine, and she picked it up and gazed at it mournfully. 'This is from two weeks ago. I wish Dinah were here—she always used to buy it and I've nothing to read now.'

'You can always buy it yourself,' Maudie pointed out.

'That's tuppence I could spend on something else.'

Freddy took the magazine from her and leafed through it. It was full of sensational stories of robbery, murder and unfortunate deaths, the bloodier the better. When he held it lightly in his hands it fell open at a story entitled 'Horrific Death On Railway Tracks'.

'She did like a real-life murder,' said Maudie sadly. 'But I don't think she ever meant to become one.'

He left them to finish their toilettes and went in search of Trenton. As usual he found him in his room, talking to Desirée.

'The girls are all very noisy this evening,' observed Trenton. 'Has one of them been offered a part or something?'

'They're excited about this story of Max D'Auberville and Loveday,' replied Freddy.

'What's that?' Desirée said.

It appeared that neither of them had seen the *Herald*, so Freddy told them the story briefly.

'Good Lord!' said Trenton. 'Was it really murder? I had no idea. And they think Max did it?'

'But why should they think that?' Desirée asked.

'Because Rupert saw him going into Loveday's dressing-room on the night Septimus died,' said Freddy.

She stared in surprise, then glanced out into the corridor, where Rupert St. Clair just happened to be passing.

'Rupert, is that true?' she said.

'What's that?' he inquired, coming into the room.

The question was repeated and explained.

'Why, yes,' he said languidly. 'To be perfectly honest I hadn't intended to say a thing about it, because it was really none of my business, but the police were *so* tiresome when Dinah died—I'd come back here for my stick, and for some reason they thought I must have throttled the girl while I was looking for it. Then they started asking about Septimus, and it seemed they'd made a connection between the two deaths. They made some most unpleasant insinuations and exasperated me so much that I simply couldn't help myself and told them what I'd seen. As a matter of fact, my first thought that night when we found Septimus dead was that Max must have given him a little tap on the head and sent him on his way, but as I say, it was none of my business, and—let's be frank about it—nobody cared a fig that Septimus had tripped off to the hereafter, so I kept my mouth shut. And then the inquest found it was an accident anyway, so I assumed I'd been mistaken and forgot about it. It was only when the police started making a nuisance of themselves that it came back to me. I like Max as much as the next man, but these flat-footed oafs are starting to get in the way, so it seemed to me the best way to get rid of them was to give them what they wanted.'

'What time was it when you saw Max?' asked Desirée. 'Can you remember?'

'Halfway through the second act. I don't know exactly what time—my watch wasn't working properly, you see, which is why I went back to my room in the first place.'

'Was it after the hornpipe?'

'Oh yes, well after that. It was when I come off during the cannibal scene.'

'Why do you ask?' said Freddy, struck by the urgency in Desirée's tone. She turned to him with a disturbed expression.

'Max can't have done it if that's when he went into Loveday's room.'

'Why not?'

'Because Septimus was already dead then. I know that because I went in myself and saw him.'

This was a revelation.

'Good God!' exclaimed Trenton.

'Well, now,' said Rupert, regarding her with interest.

'Hadn't you better tell us what happened?' said Freddy.

'I suppose I'll have to now, won't I?' She sighed. 'Very well—on the night Septimus died my light went out while I was fixing my make-up just before I went on in the second act, and at the same time I heard a heavy thump from Loveday's room next door. It was so terribly loud that I ran in to see what it was. The light was off in there too, but I could see well enough to make out Septimus lying on the floor. It was obvious he was dead. I assumed he'd been reaching for something when his light went out, and the surprise had made him overbalance and hit his head.'

'Why didn't you tell somebody?'

'I was worried there'd be an inquest and that as the person to discover his body I'd have to speak, and then my picture might be in the newspapers or the police would start looking into who I was, and Father would find me. I didn't want to appear in the story at all.' She looked uncomfortable. 'Besides, I'm afraid I went through his pockets.'

'Good God!' exclaimed Trenton again. 'Whatever for?'

'For the same reason. He had a clipping from a newspaper about my disappearance. A friend of his had come to see the show one evening and recognized me, and had sent him the article. He used to show it to me and tell me he had only to write to my father and this would all be over for me. He—he was rather unpleasant about it,' she said unhappily. 'At any rate, I'm ashamed to say my first thought was to take the thing out of his pocket so it wouldn't be found on him. I got it all right, and after that I only had a minute before I had to be onstage, so I ran to find Alf and tell him the lights had gone out then hurried into position and tried not to think about what I'd just done.'

'Good heavens, it seems as though everybody was wandering in and out of Loveday's room that night,' said Rupert. He raised an exquisite eyebrow. 'Not that that's a particularly unusual state of affairs.'

'Now, Rupert,' said Trenton.

Desirée went on:

'I waited for someone else to discover the body and kept quiet about what I'd seen for the reason I told you, and then at the inquest they said it was an accident, so I didn't think it really mattered. But if Max D'Auberville has been arrested for murder I can't keep quiet any more, can I? I can't let them hang a man for something I know he didn't do.' She frowned impatiently. 'Bother! Father won't be happy at all, and I was just starting to think I'd talked him round. I shouldn't be surprised if he starts insisting I come home again. Picking the pockets of the dead isn't considered the done thing in Northumberland—at least not in the circles we move in.'

'You were in a difficult position,' said Trenton loyally. 'I don't wonder you lost your head.'

She still looked cross.

'This is all very vexing. It's clear enough that Septimus's death really was an accident, so why did the police have to start poking around and calling it murder? I felt bad enough already about what I'd done and now it looks as though everybody will have to know about it.'

'Perhaps you might forget to tell them about the newspaper clipping,' suggested Rupert. 'There's no reason they should know about that, is there?'

'I suppose not, but they'll be angry all the same that I didn't tell them about discovering his body in the first place, and wasted their time. And then Max will find out the truth too and won't ever give me a part. I don't want to get a reputation as a trouble-maker.'

'I'm afraid this is all my fault,' said Freddy apologetically. 'Jenny found it hard to believe that Septimus died accidentally so she asked me to investigate. Then I found out that Max had been here that night and the police decided to arrest him.'

'Well, I wish they hadn't,' said Desirée.

'Besides, there still remains the question of who killed Dinah,' went on Freddy. 'Because that certainly wasn't an accident.'

'If you ask me an escaped lunatic came in and did it while everybody was changing after the show, and it has nothing to do with Septimus at all,' said Rupert.

'Perhaps you're right,' said Freddy glumly.

Chapter Twenty-One

IT APPEARED THEN that the police were no further forward
with their investigation, except that now they had a good idea
of when exactly Septimus Gooch had died, since it seemed
clear that the loud thump Desirée had heard from the room
next door was the sound of his fatal fall against the wooden
cabinet. On hearing Desirée's evidence the police were forced
to release Max D'Auberville, who swept out of the place in
high dudgeon, threatening to sue them for wrongful arrest.
Meanwhile, the press were clamouring to know why the police
had made such a mistake, and when they intended to catch
the man who had murdered Dinah Belmonte. Inspector
Entwistle was not pleased with Freddy for having sent him off
on a wild-goose chase after Max, as he saw it. Worse still, he
suspected Freddy of having given the *Herald* the story.

'Are you sure you didn't tell one of your chaps?' he
demanded, when Freddy telephoned him.

'I promise you I didn't say a word. I shouldn't have
dreamed of telling anyone after what you said—least of all the
Herald. Why, you don't think I'd have let them have the scoop
at my expense, do you?' This was not exactly calculated to
instil confidence, he realized, so he went on quickly, 'I'm

almost certain it was Loveday. She wanted her name in the paper, and this was the perfect opportunity.'

'Well I'd be ashamed to see any daughter of mine behaving like that. But whoever did it, it makes us look bad. To read all these pieces you'd think the police had no idea what they were doing. It looks like Gooch's death was an accident after all, and we're still none the wiser about who killed Dinah Belmonte. We can't get anyone on the strength of the finger-prints on the trunk, and it seems nobody at the theatre saw anything suspicious on the night she died.'

'I can go to the Jollity and ask some more questions if you like,' offered Freddy.

'Leave the investigating to the police, won't you?' replied Entwistle tersely, and hung up.

'Drat,' said Freddy. He was in a grumpy mood, for it seemed that instead of helping matters, he had somehow done nothing but get into everybody's bad books. The police thought him a meddler—and an incompetent one at that—while Max D'Auberville certainly did not look upon him favourably, given the part Freddy had played in his arrest (although one bright spot was that Freddy need no longer fear the threat of free tickets to *Consider the Ravens*). Desirée was unhappy that owing to his actions she had been forced to admit wrongdoing to the police, for her father was once more making noises about taking her home, and even the good-natured Trenton had thrown him one or two reproachful looks on her behalf. Gertie seemed to be avoiding his calls still, for which he could hardly blame her, and on top of that the weather had taken a turn for the worse, for the sunshine of the past week had been replaced by a settled rain that did little to improve his spirits. He seemed to have reached the limits of his ability to assist in the investigation. Whether Septimus had been murdered or not, there was no doubt that Dinah's death had been deliberate, and finding her killer would most likely be a matter of a painstaking sifting of finger-prints and footprints and alibis, which did not fall within his purview. Inspector Entwistle had been right, he thought—murder was best left to the police.

On Wednesday afternoon he went to the Jollity with some idea of speaking to Jenny and withdrawing from the case before he caused any more trouble. It was early still and hardly any of the cast were there, but he found that Peggy had arrived before him and was busy arranging her things in the dressing-room.

'Jenny? She's not here yet,' she informed him. 'Any news on Dinah, by the way?'

'No,' he replied. He did not add that the police were unlikely to tell him if there were, given the events of the past day or two.

'Perhaps they'll never find out who killed her,' she said sadly. 'Or what happened to Una.'

Freddy had almost forgotten about Una. That was one mystery he had never been able to fit into the picture. What *had* happened to her?

He drifted along the corridor and up to the out-of-bounds lavatory, where he stood in the doorway and gazed round, thinking. Protruding from the wall opposite, about two feet from the floor, was a short length of bare, cast-iron pipe— presumably the one the girls had whispered through when they were playing the trick on Loveday. He moved across and crouched down to examine it. Placing a hand round it to form a funnel, he put his mouth to it and said, by way of experi- ment, 'Hallo?' then put his ear to it and listened. He could hear nothing, although since Loveday had not yet arrived that was only to be expected.

He peered inside it, wondering how exactly the sound had carried from here all the way to Loveday's dressing-room on the other corridor, but although the cloak-room had a window which gave on to a back yard, the gloomy weather made it too dim to see. Freddy stood up and went to turn on the light, which cast a thin glow through the room, then went back to the pipe and put his hand to it again. A sudden, agonizing jolt of pain shot through him, causing him to snatch his arm away with a loud yelp. He swore and nursed his hand.

'What the devil—' he exclaimed.

Once he had ascertained to his satisfaction that his arm was still fully attached to his body, he approached the pipe cautiously, but without touching it, then turned his head and regarded the light switch thoughtfully. At length he turned off the light with some trepidation but without further injury, then went to find Peggy.

'Do you have that magazine of Dinah's?' he asked.

'What, this one?' She tossed it to him. 'You don't really want to read that rubbish, do you?'

He opened it and read for a minute or two, frowning.

'Don't turn the light on in the back cloak-room,' he said, shoving the magazine in his pocket, and went out without waiting for a reply. His next stop was the Calliope, where he asked to speak to Cyril Payne. Five minutes later he returned to the Jollity in company with Cyril himself.

'Hallo, Cyril,' said Peggy in surprise when she saw him. 'What are you doing here?'

'I think I know what killed Una,' said Freddy.

'Goodness! What?' she demanded.

'Come and see.'

He led the way up to the cloak-room and pointed at the pipe.

'There it is,' he said to Cyril. 'It only happened when I turned the light on.'

Cyril stepped into the room and eyed the ceiling lamp. He pointed to a line in the wall which had been roughly plastered over.

'New wiring,' he said. 'And done badly, I'm sure of it. I told them.'

He looked down. The floor was mostly laid to stone tile,

but the work had been left unfinished and the area around the pipe was little more than a patch of earth.

'That's what did it,' he said. 'If she was kneeling on that bare patch when she touched the pipe the current would have gone straight through her and into the ground.'

'What do you mean?' said Peggy.

'Una was electrocuted,' replied Freddy. 'Quite accidentally, I'd guess. She touched the pipe and got an electric shock that killed her.' He turned to Cyril. 'Do you remember I told you how the girls whispered through a pipe and pretended to be a ghost?'

Cyril was aghast.

'Here, you mean? Yes, I remember—you said it was in the new cloak-room, but I didn't make the connection at the time. I don't know why I didn't realize when you mentioned it. Nobody ought to have been using this room. I told Mr. Wilkerson the electrics were dangerous before we left, but he was all fired up because of the row with Mr. Gooch and had no time to listen to me. He'd taken on a couple of electricians who didn't know their work, you see, but they were cheap and he was all for saving money. I'm not certified myself but I know worn insulation and frayed wires when I see them, and what I saw going on sometimes made me shake my head.'

'It sounds as though Gooch and Wilkerson had a lot in common,' said Freddy. 'They both liked to do things on the cheap.'

Cyril nodded.

'I saw one of the electricians put that wiring in, and he did it slapdash, and without proper precautions. I told him but he said it didn't matter, and it would work just as well, so who was to know? A few days later Mr. Gooch and Mr. Wilkerson fell out and Wilkerson told us all to down tools and leave. If they'd patched up their differences it wouldn't have mattered much, because then we'd have come back to finish the work and I'd have made sure it was done properly. As it was, I put this sign on the door myself and told Mr. Gooch just quietly on the way out that the cloak-room wasn't safe to be used. I left Wilkerson's not long after that and to tell the truth this job fell out of my mind. If I thought of it at all I assumed Mr. Gooch must have found a different firm to finish the work, and they'd done it properly. If I'd known he hadn't I might have said something.'

He looked at the pipe, perplexed.

'But I don't understand why they didn't notice straightaway that she'd been electrocuted. Why, it would have been perfectly obvious what had happened when they found her. Mr. Gooch knew the wiring was faulty. Why didn't he speak up at the time?'

'Because she wasn't found here,' replied Freddy, carefully not looking at Peggy. 'There was some confusion when it happened, and her body was moved to her dressing-room, and that's where she was found.'

'Ah, no wonder then. It doesn't always leave any traces on the body, electrocution doesn't. Just maybe a little burn, and sometimes not even that. If they found her somewhere else it stands to reason they might not guess what had happened.'

Peggy had been listening to all this in horror.

'Oh, heavens!' she exclaimed. 'I had no idea. Why didn't anybody tell us the electrics weren't safe?'

'I expect they thought they didn't need to,' replied Freddy. 'After all, there was a sign on the door and Septimus thought his word was law. He must have thought threatening you all with the sack was enough.'

'He just said something about not getting our costumes dirty or torn—he never mentioned the place was lethal.'

'Perhaps he didn't take it seriously either, like the electrician who did the wiring.'

A thought struck her.

'But we all touched the pipe. Why didn't we get shocks too?'

'Did you have the light on?'

'No—we didn't need to in the day-time, and in the evening someone would have spotted it was on and seen what we were up to, so we did it in the dark.'

'I expect Una forgot and turned it on,' said Freddy.

'Oh, poor Una.' She had gone pale.

Cyril was examining the pipe and the plaster-work.

'At a guess I'd say an exposed wire is touching that pipe, and when the light is turned on the pipe becomes live. Just touching it would be enough to kill a person in the right circumstances.'

'Who would have thought such a little thing could do so much damage?' said Peggy.

'I can well believe it,' Freddy answered. 'It packed a punch all right. Why didn't it kill me, incidentally?'

'Rubber soles,' replied Cyril, pointing at Freddy's shoes. 'But you were lucky. If any part of your skin had been touching the ground there you'd've most likely been a goner. I expect this girl was kneeling, or if she was crouching maybe she put her hand on the floor for balance, and the current went straight through her to earth.'

'You had a lucky escape too,' said Freddy to Peggy. 'It might have happened to any one of you if the light had been on.'

Peggy wrung her hands in distress.

'And we moved her body so they never found out what had killed her. It was all our fault! Oh, Una, I'm sorry.'

'You weren't to know. It was an unlucky accident, that's all, and the only reason there was any mystery about it was because she wasn't found where she died. I take it you turned the light off before you moved her? I thought so. You might have got a shock from her if you hadn't.'

Sounds could now be heard from the stage door corridor as the other members of the cast began arriving for the matinée.

'Did you mention the wiring to Dinah?' Freddy asked Cyril.

'I seem to remember I did, yes. Why?'

'I think that's what she wanted to tell me that day—that she'd worked out what happened to Una.' He brought out Dinah's magazine from his pocket. 'Look at this.'

Cyril and Peggy peered at the page he indicated.

'Horrific Death On Railway Tracks,' read Peggy. 'Oh, I see. I thought the story was about someone being hit by a train.'

'No, it was electrocution. I rather think Dinah read this a few days before she died, remembered what Cyril had told her about the faulty wiring in the cloak-room, and started to wonder whether that was the answer. She didn't tell me that day because then she would have had to confess to the trick you'd all played on Loveday. But she told me she'd read something that made her wonder, and I reckon it was most likely this story.'

Cyril just then remembered he was supposed to be at work at the Calliope, so he went off, promising to return if his help were needed for anything else. Before he went he took out a pencil and added the word 'DANGER' in large letters to the sign on the cloak-room door.

'What are we to do now?' said Peggy. 'I mean, I suppose we'll have to admit to what we did, won't we?'

'I think it would be best. With any luck Jenny won't look upon it too harshly—after all, she has plenty of other things to worry about at present.'

'She'd have to sack three of us at once. Very well, I'll bite on the bullet and confess, but I'd better warn Minnie and Maudie first.'

Freddy coughed apologetically.

'I'm afraid I'll have to tell the police too. It's only fair to let them know that at least one mystery has been solved.'

'Oh well, if you must, you must.' She sighed. 'We're going to be in *such* trouble.'

Chapter Twenty-Two

FREDDY WENT BACK to the office and telephoned Inspector Entwistle at Scotland Yard. Entwistle was either out or—more likely—disinclined to speak to him, so he asked to speak to Sergeant Bird instead.

'Could you do me a favour, sergeant?' he said, when Bird came on the line. 'You looked at the post-mortem reports for Una Bryant and Septimus Gooch, didn't you? Do you happen to remember whether the pathologist found a burn or similar mark on either or both of the bodies?'

'Now you come to mention it, I do seem to recall there was something of the kind,' replied Bird. 'I have the reports here. Hold on a minute.'

There was the sound of paper rustling at the other end of the line. Freddy waited.

'There was a small mark on Una Bryant's right knee that might have been a graze or a burn,' said Bird at last. 'No mention of anything on Gooch that I can see.'

'I don't suppose that matters, as I gather it doesn't neces-sarily leave a trace.'

'What doesn't?'

'I know how Una died—and probably Septimus too,' said

Freddy, and explained what he had found out. 'There's no doubt that's what happened to the girl, and I'd bet my last shilling that's what killed Septimus as well. The live pipe leads through from the cloak-room to Loveday's room, where presumably it's equally live. He must have touched it and got the most tremendous shock that threw him backwards. Whether it was the shock that killed him I couldn't say, but if it wasn't that then hitting his head on that cabinet would certainly have done the trick. If you ask me, I'd say the moment the light went out in Desirée's room was the moment when it happened. If you remember, Desirée said Loveday's room was also dark when she went in and found Septimus dead. The current going through him must have caused a short-circuit that blew out the lights in those two rooms at least. Whether anyone else reported their lights going off I don't know—perhaps not, as most of them were onstage or waiting in position by that time, and Desirée reported it to Alf, who immediately went to fix it at the fuse-box.'

The sergeant let out a whistle.

'Well,' he said. 'There's a turn-up. It sounds as though you might be on to something. If I were Miss Minter I'd be thinking about bringing a suit against this Wilkerson's for negligence, since their work seems to have killed two people including her husband.'

'Yes—remind me never to hire them for any little jobs I might want doing around the house,' agreed Freddy.

'Still, that's all very well, but electricity can't explain a girl in a trunk,' Bird pointed out.

'No—that's a puzzle, all right. I'm pretty sure Dinah had deduced what happened to Una at least, if not Septimus. The question is, is there a connection between that fact and her death, or is it all just pure coincidence, and was she killed for some entirely different reason?'

'Beats me,' said Bird. 'But if you're going to try and find

out don't let Entwistle know. He's not especially pleased with you at present.'

'So I understand. I won't tread on any toes, but since I seem to be spending so much time at the Jollity lately it can't do any harm to keep my eyes and ears open.'

'Why *are* you spending so much time at the Jollity, incidentally? Are you sure you're not a stage door johnny? Some of those girls are very easy on the eyes.'

'They are indeed, but as a matter of fact this evening I shall be going there on a gentlemanly mission to inform Loveday Curtis to be careful of what she touches if she doesn't want to go flying across the room,' replied Freddy.

He had quite forgotten his intention to withdraw from the case, and was more determined than ever to solve the whole thing now that he had the answers to some of the questions that had been vexing him for so long. As soon as he could, therefore, he left the office and returned to the Jollity for the second time that day, where he was admitted to Loveday Curtis's presence. Her reaction to the news was typical of her.

'It might have been me!' she exclaimed in horror.

'Not unless you touched that pipe,' said Freddy.

'I might have done, you never know. This whole place is a death-trap! Somebody really ought to pay for this.'

Freddy forbore to point out that Septimus's death had been at least partly caused by his own parsimony.

'Then poor Septimus died accidentally after all,' she went on.

'I wonder,' said Freddy, absently. He was examining the pipes in the corner, and the one that must have killed Septimus in particular. It protruded from a spot low on the wall in the same way as the one in the back cloak-room, but was much older than that one. Freddy guessed it formed part of the original plumbing of the Jollity, which had been altered at a later date when the wash-basin had been installed, and had never been removed or properly finished off. Presumably the new water pipes at the back of the stage had been connected to this one in some way.

'Why did he touch it?' he murmured to himself. 'And why did it kill him?'

'What's that?' said Loveday, who was rooting around in among her paint bottles.

Freddy did not reply but went out in search of Peggy.

'You and Dinah used the new cloak-room on the night Septimus died, didn't you?' he said.

'Did we?'

'Yes, don't you remember? That was the night you saw Bert Spooner and thought he was a ghost.'

'I didn't really think that,' she said unconvincingly.

'Did you turn the light on?'

'No—I told you, we never turned the light on in case we got caught.'

'Are you quite sure of that?'

'Yes.'

'What about Minnie and Maudie?'

'I've no idea. I don't keep a record of everyone's visits to the lav. Why?'

'I'm wondering why the light was on that night. It must have been, or the pipe couldn't have electrocuted Septimus.'

'I can ask them if you like, but even if they didn't turn the light on, someone else might have. I assumed we were the only people using the place, but other people might have been sneaking in there too for all I know.'

'True,' he said. 'Still, that doesn't answer the question of why he touched the pipe. We know why Una touched the one in the cloak-room, but why should Septimus have put his hand on the one in Loveday's room? It's in an awkward position close to the floor—and besides, that trunk was standing in front of it at the time, if you remember.'

'Perhaps he dropped something behind the trunk and

touched the pipe accidentally when he reached down to pick it up,' she suggested.

'Perhaps. But there's another question: why did it kill him? I got a shock and didn't die because I wasn't touching bare ground at the time, unlike Una. Loveday's room is carpeted, which ought to have protected Septimus in the same way.'

'Did he have a weak heart?'

'Not according to the pathologist who examined his body.'

'Then I don't know.'

Freddy was not satisfied. There was something here that did not add up. He went to knock on Jenny's door.

'Mind the trunk,' she said, as the door knocked against something. He squeezed in and found that the very trunk he had just been talking about was taking up most of the few valuable square feet of floor available in the room. Jenny was in front of the glass, putting the finishing touches to her hair.

'This trunk seems to move about rather a lot,' observed Freddy.

'The police have just brought it back,' she replied. 'I don't know why they left it in here for us to trip over. You'd think they'd have noticed this is one of the smallest rooms on the corridor.' She regarded it with distaste. 'I don't think we can ever use it again after what happened. I'll never be able to forget what it was used for. Perhaps we might sell it and buy a new one. It's very old and battered now anyway. By the way, I suppose you know what the chorus have been getting up to?'

It seemed Peggy and the twins had confessed and thrown themselves on her mercy that afternoon.

'What makes it worse is that it's obviously the faulty wiring that killed Septimus too,' she said. 'I told you he wouldn't have fallen just like that, didn't I? But an electric shock would certainly explain it. The girls feel awful about it, because if they'd spoken up then we'd have had the thing fixed and Septimus wouldn't have been killed. But as I pointed out to them, Septimus knew perfectly well about the danger and didn't say anything either—or pay to have it put right—so I suppose you might say it was partly his own fault. And if he'd mentioned it perhaps Una would still be alive too.'

'You're not going to sack them, then?'

'Do you think I ought to? It seems to have been one unfortunate coincidence after another. Of course they oughtn't to have been playing that joke on Loveday, but Una paid for it dearly, so I can't really find it in my heart to punish them further.'

'Does Loveday know about the joke?'

'Goodness, no! I told them not to confess to her under any circumstances. Can you imagine the fuss she'd make? I have quite enough on my plate without that. Still,' she went on, 'at least Septimus wasn't murdered. We'll get an electrician in as a matter of urgency to fix the fault and leave the police to concentrate on finding out who killed poor Dinah. The more I think about it, the more I'm convinced it was someone quite unknown who came in and did it while we were all busy.'

Freddy thought she was deluding herself, but did not tell her so. He gazed absently at the trunk, for he was still pondering the question of what could have caused Septimus to touch the lethal pipe in Loveday's dressing-room when the trunk had been standing in front of it. As he did so, a memory flitted suddenly through his mind. He squatted down and began to examine the trunk closely.

'What are you doing?' Jenny asked.

'I pulled a thread on a perfectly good jacket when it caught on this a few days ago.' He gave a triumphant exclamation. 'And this is why.'

She came closer to look and he pointed out the thing he was looking at. It was a tiny fragment of copper wire that was caught in the hinge of one of the catches.

'Better not touch it,' he said.

'What is it?'

'Murder, if I'm not much mistaken,' he said grimly.

'I don't understand.'

'I'm not sure I do myself, but I know a man who can help us.'

She was looking at him in astonishment.

'You think Septimus really was murdered, then? But who did it?'

'I rather think it's obvious *who* did it,' said Freddy. 'The question is: why?'

———

BERT SPOONER WAS in Trenton and Jinks's dressing-room when Freddy went in, sitting in the armchair and reading the *Sporting Times*. He was even more morose than Jinks if possible, and the two of them were conversing in grunts, insofar as they spoke at all.

'Hallo, Freddy,' said Trenton cheerfully. 'Still snooping around?'

'More or less.'

'We're all celebrating this evening, because Jinks and Spooner are going to America,' Trenton said.

Jinks and Spooner did not look particularly as though they were celebrating.

'Congratulations,' said Freddy. 'When are you off?'

'Three weeks' time,' replied Jinks with grim satisfaction. 'I can't wait to get out of this god-forsaken place.'

'Didn't the police make any difficulty?'

'About what? Dinah, you mean? Bert had nothing to do with it and they can't prove he did,' Jinks said, as Spooner shook his newspaper in agreement.

Freddy went to look idly at the photographs on the walls, his mind still turning over the conversation he had just had with Jenny, but his attention was soon caught by how strange all the performers looked in their odd costumes of a quarter of a century ago. Even the names were those of a bygone era:

Sylvester Ramsbottom and his unicycle, The Great Alphonso, Jacinta Moreno. He said the last name out loud, for he was sure he had heard it before.

'Jacinta Moreno? That's Jenny,' said Trenton, coming to join him.

'Oh, of course. That was her stage name many years ago, wasn't it?' Freddy looked closer. 'My word, she was a beauty in those days. Now, where do I know this chap from?'

He examined a photograph closely for several moments, then started.

'Good Lord!' he murmured to himself. 'Why didn't I notice before? He did mention it, now I come to think of it.'

Trenton was not listening, for he was looking at something else.

'Here's a photo of Septimus and Jenny in 1906,' he said, indicating. 'Septimus is looking rather pleased with himself.'

'I expect he was,' said Spooner without raising his head from his paper. 'He'd just burned his theatre down and claimed on the insurance, hadn't he?'

Freddy turned to look at him, surprised.

'What's that? He didn't really burn it down deliberately, did he?'

Spooner shrugged.

'I dunno. That's what he said, but it might have been an idle boast. He was the type.'

'He told you that?'

'Not me. I overheard him talking to Alf about it. They came in one morning when I'd been sleeping on the sofa in the girls' room and caught me unawares. I had to hide in the cupboard sharpish. He just mentioned it in passing, as if everybody knew already, although it was the first I'd heard of it. It's not exactly a surprise though—he was a real old twister.'

'Does Jenny know about this?'

'Who knows? Maybe she did but didn't want to say anything out of loyalty.'

Freddy was thinking rapidly. Was this the explanation he had been looking for? He went out into the corridor.

'Minnie,' he said to a passing twin.

'I'm Maudie,' she replied.

'Maudie, then. Did you tell anybody about where you really found Una? Or did you keep it to yourselves?'

She eyed him sideways.

'I don't want to get anyone into trouble,' she said.

Freddy gave her a name and she hesitated, then nodded.

'Yes. Why?'

'Just wondering. Thanks.'

'You're welcome. I was only kidding by the way—I am Minnie,' she said, and went off with a wink. Freddy shook his head.

The cast were now coming out of their dressing-rooms, ready to take their positions. Freddy looked for Jenny, wanting to speak to her, but was informed that she had already gone onstage with Desirée. All would be confusion from now until the end of the show—and besides, nothing further could be done until he could get hold of Cyril, who would have gone home for the day. He scribbled a note and left it in a prominent position in Jenny's dressing-room, where nothing could accidentally be put on top of it, then went home.

Chapter Twenty-Three

WHEN FREDDY ARRIVED at the Jollity at ten the next morning he found that Jenny had already arrived in reply to his summons and was waiting for him in Loveday's dressing-room.

'What is it you wanted to show me?' she asked.

'I don't know exactly, until Cyril arrives,' he replied. 'But in the meantime, we may as well set the scene. We'll need that trunk. Is it still in your room?'

He went out and returned with the article in question, which he set down on its end in the same position in which it had been found on the night of Septimus's death.

'Can you remember how it was, exactly? I know it was open like this.' He snapped the catches and opened the trunk fully, then pushed it into place so that the inside was facing them.

'The top two drawers were open,' she said.

'Yes, they were, weren't they?' He pulled them open, then stepped back to regard his handiwork. 'Have I missed anything? Is this how the room looked when we found Septimus?'

'I think so.'

'Now, I don't know how to set up an electrical booby-trap myself, but I expect we'll need some copper wire. Luckily for our murderer there's some lying around handy in the props room. I saw it the other week and didn't realize it was important. I'll leave it there for now, though, as it may have fingerprints on it—and besides, I'm hoping Cyril will bring something with him that's less dangerous. He ought to be here soon. What shall we do while we wait? I've a fancy for some music.'

He went out again and came back with the gramophone from the props room.

'You've found the gramophone! I'd been looking for that. Where was it?' said Jenny, as he put it down on a chair. She took up the record that lay on the turntable and looked at it. 'Goodness, I haven't heard this song in years. I'd quite forgotten about it. The Great Alphonso. How things have changed since then!'

'You sang with him a long time ago, didn't you? I mean, back in the days of the original Jollity Theatre.'

'Yes. It was an awful pity what happened. He was a remarkable talent.'

Just then they heard the sound of someone arriving at the theatre and shortly afterwards Cyril Payne appeared, carrying a bag of tools.

'This is how the room looked that night, Cyril,' said Freddy, indicating the trunk. 'What do you think?'

Cyril regarded the trunk with a professional air.

'There's plenty of metal on it, with all that banding and those studs.' Resting his hands on it, he leaned over and looked down the back of it. 'And that's the pipe.' He stepped back and looked around, and his gaze fell on a narrow iron radiator on the wall to the right of the wash-basin. 'That radiator there would do the trick, I dare say.'

'I wondered about the radiator,' said Freddy.

Cyril opened his bag and brought out several lengths of insulated wire.

'I'm not risking bare copper,' he said. 'I suppose the cloak-room light isn't turned on? Good. Now, let's see…'

He shifted the trunk out of the way and set to work. Freddy and Jenny watched curiously as he stripped the insulation from one end of a length of wire and wrapped it firmly around the protruding pipe.

'Now, we lead it from the pipe to somewhere on this side of the trunk,' he said.

'There's a bit of wire caught in that catch there—probably from the original trap,' said Freddy. 'Better attach this piece to something else, as the police will want to look at it.'

'I'll use this catch instead.' Cyril busied himself with a pair of pliers. 'There. Now we lead another wire from the other open side of the trunk to earth, or in this case, the radiator.'

He suited the action to the word.

'You see? The wire from the pipe to one side of the trunk forms one part of the circuit, and the wire from the other side of the trunk to the radiator forms another part. It's easy enough to push both wires out of sight behind the trunk itself so they wouldn't be spotted. But for the circuit to be completed they need to connect in the middle. Let's try it.'

Cyril took two more short lengths of wire and attached one to one open side of the trunk and another to the other side. Then he removed the light bulb from the ceiling lamp and wrapped both wires around it.

'I wouldn't do this if the light in the cloak-room was on,' he said. 'This is our circuit. Now, I'm going to turn the light on, which will send a current through the pipe. Watch—and whatever you do, don't touch anything!'

He went out and they heard him retreating along the corridor. After a moment they heard his voice call 'Ready', and a second later there was a buzzing sound and the bulb lit up.

'Oh!' exclaimed Jenny.

'Did it work?' said Cyril, as he came back in.

'I'll say,' replied Freddy. 'That clinches it, I think. Replace the light bulb with a human being and you've got a nasty accident—or a murder in this case.'

'But why the trunk?' asked Jenny, as Cyril, ever mindful of safety and proper procedure, left the room again to turn the light off.

'The problem was that our murderer needed Septimus to touch the pipe,' Freddy explained. 'It was easy enough to make him go and look at it, but there was no way of guaranteeing he would touch it—or that it would kill him if he did, since the carpet would have protected him. So the killer rigged up this trap instead.'

'How did he make him go and look at the pipe?'

'Why, he simply told Septimus about the trick the girls played on Loveday, then went to demonstrate. He told Septimus to listen for a voice coming from the corner of the dressing-room, then went to the back cloak-room to show him the trick. He turned on the light, which made the pipe live and set the trap. Our murderer called through the pipe, being careful not to touch it, then left the trap to do its work.

'Now, if you heard a voice coming from this corner of the room, what would be the natural thing to do? You'd go across and listen to find out where the sound was coming from, wouldn't you? But the trunk is in the way, so what do you do? You put one hand on this side of it and one hand on that side and lean over it to get a better look at the pipe. You saw Cyril do it just now, in fact, when he came in. As your hands touch the metal your body forms the final link in the circuit and before you know it—bang!—two hundred and forty volts shoot through you and hurl you backwards across the room. If you look at the trunk you'll see it's positioned very carefully, so you'd be bound to put one hand on either side of it if you wanted to peer over it. And that's exactly what Septimus did.

From our murderer's point of view it came off beautifully, and all he had to do to hide his traces was to remove a couple of wires in all the confusion over the finding of the body.'

'I can hardly believe it,' said Jenny. 'But what do we do now?'

'We leave it to the police,' replied Freddy. 'I telephoned them before I came, and I expect they'll be here soon.'

'What's all this, then?' came a voice from the doorway, and they turned to see Alf regarding the scene with surprise. When he spotted Cyril, who had just returned and was winding a length of wire into a coil, a wary look came across his face.

'We've found out, Alf,' said Freddy. 'Why did you do it? Was it the fire?'

Alf did not answer for a moment. His eye fell on the gramophone and he came into the room and wound it up. The sweet strains of the song Freddy and Dinah had heard that day at the theatre filled the air, and they listened, spellbound.

'I was the greatest,' he said at last. 'I was, wasn't I, Jen?'

'Yes, you were, Alf.'

'I never wanted to do anything else but be on the stage. From three years old I was on the boards, doing tumbling tricks for anyone who'd watch. All the music halls, I played— the Holborn Varieties, the Canterbury, the Alhambra. But when I grew up it was singing I liked. And I had the voice for it—none sweeter. You can keep your Rupert St. Clairs—he couldn't hold a candle to how I was at my best. I could move people to tears when I liked. The Great Alphonso, I called myself—better than plain old Alf Potts. I was nothing at first, but I was ambitious and knew what I wanted. So I worked hard and people began to talk about me, and then almost before I knew it I was a name in London and getting offers from all the big managers. I made records, and they sold sheet music with my picture on it and put stories about me in the paper, and people stopped me in the street and asked for my autograph. I even sang for the Queen. When they started talking about me as the next Caruso I knew nothing could stop me. Those were good times.

'The women liked me too, although there was just one I wanted. But she had her eye on another man, and since I was on my way up and the jobs were coming in thick and fast and I had other things to keep me occupied, I didn't stand in her way. I knew the man she liked was a villain, but what could I do?'

'Oh, Alf,' said Jenny sadly.

He waved a hand.

'Well, never mind that. We don't always get what we want, do we? I found that out twice over. Pride goes before a fall, they say. I thought I was heading for the top, until it all collapsed around my ears.'

He stared wistfully at the gramophone.

'I can't tell you how many times over the years I've re-lived that night. If only I hadn't fallen asleep after the performance it never would have happened. But I'd been working hard as a favour to Septimus. He'd just bought the Jollity, you see. It was an old theatre that had fallen into disrepair, and he wanted to bring it back to the way it was, so he asked me to do some concerts to help him raise the funds. I was a big enough draw by then to make him a lot of money quickly. I agreed to do it —not for his sake, but for Jen's. I didn't know it at the time, but it seems he couldn't wait to do things the usual way and had a short-cut in mind.'

'An insurance claim,' said Freddy.

Alf nodded.

'I don't suppose he knew I was inside, and I don't suppose he'd have cared if he had. He was all for the money and hang the people who brought it in for him. Or perhaps he did know, and wanted to rub it in and teach me a lesson for having dared to look at Jenny. We'll never know now, will we?

'We'd had a run of hot weather and the whole building was as dry as tinder. Went up a treat, it did,' he said ironically. 'I got out, but not before I'd had a good few lungfuls of red-hot ash and smoke. I could hardly breathe for weeks, and when my voice came back it was nothing more than a whisper at first. I rested it, as they told me, and waited and hoped, but it was never the same again. I couldn't sing a note in anything more than a croak, and the range was all gone. I saw the best doctors in the business and they all shrugged their shoulders and said there was nothing to be done.

'So that was that. They put the fire down to an accident, and that's what I believed. Septimus got a brand new theatre out of the insurance money, put on one show after another and got rich. But for me it was all over. The agents and the producers didn't want to know me, the work dried up, and nobody wanted my autograph any more. The Great Alphonso was dead—or might as well have been. All those years of hard work, up in smoke in less than an hour. And if I couldn't sing, what else could I do? Without a voice I couldn't act either and I was too old to go back to tumbling. But I had to be in the theatre somehow—it was all I'd ever known, so in the end I stayed here at the Jollity on the stage door. It wasn't the same as being on the stage, but it was the nearest I was ever likely to get.

'Twenty-five years I worked for him, letting people in and out of the theatre, watching young singers work their way up from nothing to being famous, just like I did, and always thinking that it ought to have been me. They never noticed me —and why should they have? I was just old Alf who took letters and flowers in for them and fetched things and fixed things for them. Twenty-five years I believed it was all because of an accident, and I might have gone to the grave believing it if he hadn't let it slip himself a few weeks ago.

'He was talking about how he'd got the cheapest insurance he could for the tour of the provinces. Insurance men were fools, he said. If he was running an insurance company he'd never pay out a penny on a claim until he'd made damn' sure they weren't trying to put one over on him, because you could be certain that half the world was trying to take the other half for a sucker—and he should know. I asked him what he meant, and he said, "Where do you think the money came from for this theatre? A nice little accident, wasn't it? And it came just at the right time. Not that they'll ever prove a thing against me."

'He laughed when he said it, just as if it was nothing! A life ruined and he didn't even have the decency to remember it, because of course he wouldn't have told me what he'd done if he'd kept it in mind, would he?'

His brow lowered in anger as he remembered.

'So you decided to kill him,' said Freddy. 'How did you come up with the plan?'

'I could have struck him down then and there—well, except he's bigger than I am so there wouldn't have been much use in that. But I knew I couldn't stand to breathe the same air as him for much longer, so I started doing some thinking. I could have stuck a knife in him or shot him or anything you like, but then I remembered Jen. You were always good to me,' he said to her. 'I didn't want to give Septimus the satisfaction of me getting caught, but if the police didn't get me then they might fasten on you or someone else, and I didn't want that either.

'I was still determined to get him back, but I didn't know how to do it until after young Una died. I knew the girls had been playing a joke on that pert little miss who thinks she's above everyone else, and whispering through the pipes at her, but I didn't make the connection between the trick and Una's death at the time because they'd moved her body to their dressing-room so as to keep out of trouble.

'Then one morning when there was nobody else in the theatre I happened to go into the cloak-room and turn the light on, heard a bang, and found that one of the lights in the stage door corridor had gone out. I did some poking about and got a shock from the pipe that nearly sent me through the wall. It didn't take too long for me to put two and two together about what had killed Una, and it was obvious somebody must have moved her, so I asked those minxes of twins and they admitted to it. I didn't mention the electrics to them, because that's when I got the idea of how to get rid of Septimus. I knew I could rig something up, and I thought it couldn't do any harm to give it a try. So I wired up the trunk and waited for my opportunity. It might have worked, or it might not have. But if it did I thought it would serve him right twice—once for me and once for Una, because if he hadn't been so tight-fisted he'd have had those electrics fixed in the first place and she'd never have been killed.'

'I saw you talking to Septimus that night just before he died. Then you wandered off to the back corridor,' said Freddy.

Alf nodded.

'The beauty of the whole thing was that nobody needed to be there. All I had to do was switch a light on and call through a pipe, and the trunk would do the rest. Well, I had my satisfaction, all right. Funny, it didn't feel as good as I thought it would.'

Jenny had been listening, her face desolate.

'What about Dinah?' she said. 'Did you kill her too? But why, Alf?'

His face darkened.

'I didn't mean to, Jen,' he said. 'Honest, I didn't. She must've worked out what killed Una. I came into the cloak-room that night after the show and found her in her evening-dress, crouching on the floor and squinting at the pipe, with the light on. "Don't touch it!" I said. "It's dangerous." "Then it *was* electrocution that killed her," she said. "We must tell Jenny." And then I saw her thinking. "But Alf, this pipe leads through to Loveday's room," she said. "Do you think that's what killed Mr. Gooch too?" "I doubt it," I said, trying to steer her away from the idea. But she wasn't stupid. "It must be," she said. "Oh, Alf, we can't keep it quiet any longer—this place is dangerous. I'm going to tell the girls we must confess what we did."

'She was talking in a raised voice and there were still a few people left in the theatre, so I must have panicked. If it was found out that he'd been electrocuted they'd have remembered the trunk and realized it couldn't have been an accident. Or at least, that was what I thought. So I put my hand over her mouth to quiet her—I swear all I wanted to do was make her hush for a few minutes to give me time to think. But perhaps I did it a bit too harsh, not meaning to, because she started to struggle and panic, and the next thing I knew she was dead on the floor in front of me.

'Lucky for me the rest of the people left a few minutes later, but I knew Bert Spooner would be back any second and I didn't want him catching me with a dead body so I put her in the trunk, meaning to come back the next day when he was out, and move her somewhere else. Rupert came back for his stick while I was carrying her along the corridor to the props room and gave me a nasty moment, but lucky for me he didn't see me at it. Then you found her before I had the chance to come back and hide her properly,' he said to Freddy. 'She was a nice little thing,' he finished sadly.

There was a silence as they all digested what had just been said, and looked at the wiry little man whose chance of fame and fortune had been ruined by the greed and carelessness of his employer, and who had at last taken the ultimate revenge.

'The police will be here shortly,' said Jenny at last.

Alf nodded.

'I can wait. I'll take what's coming to me.'

He wound up the gramophone again, to listen one last time to the sound of the beautiful voice he had had and lost.

As he stared unseeing, lost in the memory of the past, two tears rolled down his cheeks and they all looked away.

Soon afterwards the police arrived and Alf pulled himself together.

'Here you are, then. I suppose you'd better take me away.' He turned to Jenny and gave her a wry look. 'My final performance. How did I do?'

'You brought the house down,' said Jenny.

'You're a good girl, Jen,' he said as he was led away.

Chapter Twenty-Four

'OF COURSE THERE WAS TALK,' said Jenny, much later. 'But I swear Septimus never confessed anything of the sort to me. Do you think I'd have stood by and said nothing if I'd known he burnt his own theatre down? I thought it was an unlucky accident, like everyone else.' She sighed. 'Poor Alf. We sang together many times in the old days. He wasn't exaggerating, you know—he was the sweetest singer I've ever heard. And tremendously good-looking. All the girls were in love with him —including me, for a little while. He could have been world-famous—I remember they'd been planning a European tour when the accident happened, but of course it never came off in the end. What made you suspect him?'

'Oh, nothing, really—just the little bits of information I picked up here and there,' replied Freddy. 'Before I knew about the booby-trap, it was clear that the only two members of the cast who could possibly have had the time to kill Septimus were Desirée and Rupert, since you, Trenton, Loveday and Morry Jinks don't come offstage long enough to have done it. Loveday does all her changes in the wings, while Trenton comes off briefly several times and doesn't do any changes at all. You and Jinks both come off to change, but it simply wouldn't have been possible for either of you to change *and* kill Septimus in the time available. Desirée, on the other hand, doesn't go onstage immediately, and was out of sight for the first few minutes of the second act, while Rupert was late and nearly missed his cue. Of course, we know now what Desirée was doing during those few minutes —and besides, I didn't see how she could have knocked Septimus over. I did consider Rupert for a while, but once I knew about the electrical fault and had deduced it was a deliberate trap, then it was obvious it must have been someone who was the handy sort—which doesn't exactly sound like Rupert. But Alf was here most of the time, knew the theatre like the back of his hand, and knew where to lay his hands on some copper wire and the trunk. When I found out that the twins had confessed to him about having moved Una's body, it seemed likely that he'd worked out how she died and got the idea from that. And when I thought about Desirée's light going out, I was even more sure. If you remember, she reported it to Alf who immediately went to turn the lights back on at the fuse-box, but surely it would have been more natural to look in all the rooms first and see where the problem was? Of course, he knew perfectly well why the lights had blown out and how to fix them, so he didn't bother.'

'Clever of you.'

'Not really. I'd never have figured the thing out at all if I hadn't touched the pipe and got a shock myself. As for Dinah, Alf was the last to leave the theatre that night. If somebody else had strangled her there was every chance they would have been seen, but Alf's having been there after everyone else had gone made it more likely that he was the one who did it. He locked up at shortly after eleven—by which time Dinah must surely have been dead and in the trunk or she'd have been on her way to the party by then—and Spooner didn't turn up until a while after Alf had gone, so he was unlikely to be the murderer, as why would Alf have left her still alive in the theatre?

'Even then, once I suspected a trap and realized Alf had probably laid it, and must therefore also have killed Dinah, I had no idea why he should have wanted to kill Septimus. It was quite a coincidence that I recognized him in the photograph in Trenton's room just as Bert Spooner was telling me he'd overheard Septimus confessing to Alf about having burned the theatre down. I was curious, so I went and looked through the archives of the *Clarion*, and discovered the fate of The Great Alphonso. It was reported quite widely at the time, although it soon faded from public memory. The abrupt and brutal ending of a potentially glorious career seemed like a good enough motive for murder to me, and so it was.'

'I shall pay for his defence, naturally,' she said gloomily. 'Oh dear, what a difficult few weeks it's been! I'll be pleased when we go on the road at last. I think we all need to get away from London for a while. This theatre feels unlucky just now. Perhaps I'll sell it and start afresh somewhere else.'

Freddy was expected elsewhere, so he made his excuses, leaving her ruminating over her future business plans. He found Gertie sitting by the Serpentine and joined her on the seat.

'How was Norfolk?' he said.

'Dull, as usual. Filthy weather. I ran the car into a ditch.'

'Again? Any injuries?'

'No more than usual.'

She was staring broodily at the lake.

'Listen, I didn't have a chance to explain about the other day,' he began, but she waved a hand.

'There's no need.' She turned to face him. 'As a matter of fact, that's what I wanted to talk to you about.'

'I promise you I haven't been misbehaving,' he said, entirely untruthfully.

'That's just it. I don't care.'

'What?'

'I've caught you draped in pretty girls who can do back-somersaults three or four times in the past fortnight, and it didn't bother me at all. That can't be a good thing, can it?'

Freddy thought it was a very good thing.

'Why not?' he wanted to know.

'Because it means I'm not in love with you. Oh, I thought I was, for about five minutes in the summer, but I can't have been, can I? Or I'd have been upset at finding those girls hiding in your bedroom. But I just thought it was all rather amusing. You ought to have seen your face when I opened that door!' She laughed at the memory. 'I thought you were going to take a header out of the window to escape.'

'I suppose it was rather funny,' admitted Freddy.

'It was. And it made me realize we should end it. You don't mind, do you? I mean, you're not especially unhappy about it?'

'No,' said Freddy, perhaps a little rashly.

'We're much better off as pals. We are good pals, aren't we? We have lots of fun together, and we can keep doing that for as long as you like. But you must set me free to love again,' she declaimed sententiously.

'All right.'

'I expect I'll marry you one day,' she went on. 'You can be my third husband. My first will be some elderly and achingly tedious Earl or Viscount that Father approves of, then once I've buried him and inherited all his money I'll fall madly in love with a completely unsuitable adventurer and utter cad, who'll fleece me then die in a plane crash. A year after that you and I will meet accidentally after many years apart. You'll be nursing a broken heart because whichever woman you've been chasing has moved to Argentina with her husband, and we'll marry each other on the rebound and live happily for the rest of our days.'

'You have this all planned, do you?'

'It's as well to be prepared.' She looked at him and laughed again. 'You did look funny in that grass skirt. And twins! I'd like some twins too. I was thinking of those—what's the name? Stokerton, is it? You remember them. They were at your mother's big party last year.'

'Cuthbert and Wilfred? The Piglets, we called them at school, because they squealed whenever you kicked them. You don't want them, they're ghastly—they've got knock knees and their ears stick out at right-angles. And I happen to know…'

He whispered something in her ear and her eyes widened.

'Well, I don't think I'd like that,' she said doubtfully. 'Scratch twins, then. But I shall outdo you somehow.'

'You're supposed to be a respectable young lady. Go and marry old Biffy.'

'Biffy? He *has* been giving me certain looks. I wonder what it's like to step out with a normal person.'

'Why don't you give it a try?'

'Perhaps I shall.'

'You're a sport, Gertie,' said Freddy.

'I know,' she replied.

———

Ten days later Freddy returned to the stage door of the Jollity and was admitted by a man he did not recognize who positively bristled with efficiency. Jenny Minter was in her room as usual.

'Where's Desirée?' he asked.

'In the room opposite,' she replied. 'The big dressing-room on the back corridor is finished and the chorus have moved back into it, so that's freed up two rooms down here. Trenton and Jinks don't have to share any more and nor do Desirée and I.'

'I take it they've fixed the wiring.'

'Yes. The new builder took one look at it and went very white in the face. He says it's a wonder we weren't all killed.'

'What about Wilkerson's? Any luck with them?'

She grimaced.

'Apparently they've stopped trading. It's hardly a surprise, I suppose. I'll see what I can do, but somehow I doubt whether we'll ever get anything out of them. Is it even worth wasting my time on it, I wonder? I've the tour to think about, and the thought of engaging in a fruitless chase after a shifty builder doesn't exactly appeal.'

'Ah, yes, the tour. How are things progressing?'

'It's all coming together nicely, despite everything. Have you heard Loveday is deserting us?'

'Not really? For Max D'Auberville?'

'No, she decided at the last minute not to sign her contract for the tour and accepted the lead in *Meet Me At Six*, Vernon Hughes's latest at the Emperor Theatre. It's a bigger production than this one, and she'll have a much larger dressing-room, which ought to make her happy.'

'Max must be devastated.'

'I rather think he's relieved. He's busy writing a sequel to *Consider the Ravens* and wants me to fund it. I've said I'll think about it.'

'Who's going to take Loveday's part in *Have At It!*, then?' asked Freddy. 'Desirée, I assume.'

'Yes. She's tremendously nervous, but I know she'll do a splendid job. I don't think her father is too pleased, but I've promised we'll look after her. I talk relentlessly about all the titled girls I was at school with and their husbands, and that seems to calm him. I think the tour will go well. Rupert has agreed to join us, which will be good for business. He can't quite hit the notes these days, but he's such a draw it oughtn't to matter. We can change things around a little in his big number, and take it down a key or two if necessary.'

Freddy left her fussing over lists of things to do, and went out into the corridor. Everything seemed so normal it was almost impossible to believe that two murders had taken place here.

'No, you can't come in,' the new door-keeper was saying to a harassed-looking young man. 'But I can pass on a message. Which Miss Monteith was it that you wanted? Minnie or Maudie?'

'Why, I don't quite know,' replied the man hesitantly.

Freddy put his head in at Trenton's door to say hallo, then turned to see Peggy just coming down from the back corridor.

'Don't tell me someone else has died,' she said.

'Not that I know of. No, I just came to see how everyone is getting along. I hear Loveday is taking her talents elsewhere.'

'Yes, she's going to Vernon Hughes. Don't ask me how she got the part if you don't want to hear me say something uncharitable. I imagine Vernon's wife will be watching her like a hawk, though.'

'You're not disappointed that they're giving the lead to Desirée, are you?'

She beamed.

'No, I like Desirée—and besides, they've given me her part for the tour!'

'I say, congratulations!'

'It's a start,' she said. 'You'll see my name at the top of the bill one day. Are you going to stay and watch the show?'

'Yes, but from the front this time. I have a ticket.'

'Didn't your girl-friend want to come?'

'She isn't my girl-friend any more. Well, not in that way, anyway.'

'Oh dear, I hope it wasn't our fault.'

'Not exactly,' said Freddy.

'Never mind, you'll find someone else soon. You don't look the type to go very long without a girl on your arm.' She eyed him for a moment. 'In fact, you can take me out if you like,' she said lightly.

He looked up in surprise.

'I'll be leaving for the tour soon so you wouldn't have to commit yourself for long,' she went on. 'What do you think? I like to go to the theatre too, even if it is a busman's holiday for me.'

'Why not? What should you like to see?' he said.

She hesitated.

'You might think it's odd, but I'd like to go and see *Consider the Ravens*. Nobody else will come and see it with me as they think it's too la-di-da, but I quite like plays that make me think. But we don't have to if you think it's an awful bore,' she added hurriedly.

Freddy looked at her. She was smiling at him. It was a nice smile. She was a pretty girl.

'I should be delighted,' he said.

————

Acknowledgments

My sincere thanks go to Peter Mason, without whose ideas and expertise I could not have laid my trail of death and destruction. Any mistakes are, of course, my own.

Books by Clara Benson

THE ANGELA MARCHMONT MYSTERIES

THE FREDDY PILKINGTON-SOAMES ADVENTURES

SHORT STORIES

Angela's Christmas Adventure

The Man on the Train

A Question of Hats

A Pinch of Strychnine

COLLECTIONS

Angela Marchmont Mysteries Books 1-3

Angela Marchmont Mysteries Books 4-6

Freddy Pilkington-Soames Adventures Books 1-3

OTHER

The Lucases of Lucas Lodge

In Darkness, Look for Stars

The Stolen Letter

Made in the USA
Coppell, TX
16 May 2022